THE ROCKER WHO HATES ME

OTHERWORLD

USA TODAY BEST SELLING AUTHOR

TERRI ANNE BROWNING

1st Edition Published June 2015
Published by Terri Anne Browning
Written By Terri Anne Browning
Edited by Lorelei Logsdon
Photo by Shauna Kruse at Kruse Images & Photography
Cover Design by Rachel Mizer at Shoutlines Design
Models Lance Jones and Jurnee Lane
Formatting by IndieVention Designs

ISBN-13: 978-1514304860
ISBN-10: 1514304864

10 9 8 7 6 5 4 3 2 1

Dedication

To all the fans that championed Gabriella Moreitti
from the very beginning.
This one is for you.

TABLE OF CONTENTS

Gabriella

The humid northern California air was starting to cool as the night wore on. I grimaced as I pulled the phone from my ear and stared at it, wishing I could see my cousin on the other end. I should have FaceTimed with her so that I could see her face. Alexis was always at her most beautiful when she was pissed off.

"Have you lost your frigging mind, Gabs?" Alexis practically shouted and I could still hear her clearly even with the phone an arms-length away from my ear. "Why are you doing this to yourself again? He's an idiot. Liam Bryant is not worth your time."

I blew out a frustrated sigh and glared up at the star-filled night sky. The rock festival I'd wormed my way into was drawing to an end for the night. OtherWorld was on stage at the moment and then Demon's Wings would close the place down. I wasn't sure how my manager had gotten me onto the lineup for this event, especially with only a few days to do it, but I was grateful that she'd worked her magic.

I'd already performed earlier in the day on one of the smaller stages, so I didn't have to worry about work getting in the way of the real reason I was there. My band and the few members of my road crew could deal with anything that needed immediate attention for now.

"Lee-Lee, stop," I commanded. She had no room to judge what I was doing, not when I'd once said the same thing about the man who was now her husband. "I'm where I need to be. You don't know what is going on with me and Liam, so just stop. Nonno…" My voice broke as memory after memory of my grandfather flowed through my mind and I had to clear my throat. "He confessed something to me last week, Lee-Lee."

That had my beautiful cousin pausing and I heard her breath hitch. Our grandfather had had a major heart attack the week before and had only lasted a few days afterwards. I'd suspected he'd only hung on as long as he had so that he could clear his conscious. What he'd confessed to me, the things that he'd admitted to doing, would have made me hate him if I hadn't known that he wasn't going to make it.

It had taken a lot more strength than I had even known I possessed to forgive that old man, but I hadn't wanted him to die thinking that I hated him. *I* hadn't wanted to live with the guilt of letting him think it.

"Wh-what did he tell you?" Alexis whispered. My beloved cousin had had a rocky relationship with our grandfather for most of her life. Alexis had been born illegitimately and the old-world Italian man hadn't let her live that down. She'd always tried so hard—sometimes too hard—to gain his respect. It wasn't until she had nearly died that he had finally realized she meant so much to him.

"I don't want to get into it right now, Lee-Lee." I would be there all night if I went into the last conversation I'd ever had with my *Nonno*. "I just called you to let you know I wouldn't be able to get Jordan this weekend like I'd promised him." I pushed my hair out of my face and leaned back against my tour bus.

If Annabelle hadn't been able to get me this gig today, I would have been back in Malibu getting ready to spend the weekend with the little man who owned my heart just as much as his mother did. Alexis's son was a miracle, and I usually never wasted the chance to get to spend time with him. But this time, something was more important.

I needed to talk to Liam. Since he wasn't returning my calls or responding to any of the hundred-plus emails that I'd sent him in the last week, he'd left me no other choice. As soon as he got off the stage, I was going to corner him and make him tell me the truth. Make him admit that he still loved me as much as I loved him. Make him tell me that he wanted to be with me. Then, if he didn't ask the question that mattered the most, I would do the asking. We'd already wasted too much time and I wasn't going to waste another minute.

I was going to marry Liam Bryant. He just didn't know it yet.

Alexis blew out a frustrated sigh and I couldn't help but smile. "Okay. Just know that I love you, Gabs. No matter what happens with you and Liam, I'm here for you."

"I love you too, Lee-Lee."

I could hear OtherWorld ending their show and quickly said goodbye to my cousin. With the end of our connection, I lost some of my confidence. I needed to do this—for me, but also for Liam. That didn't mean I wasn't terrified that he would continue to push me out of his life.

My grandfather had filled Liam's head full of all kinds of nonsense in an attempt to protect me from a man he'd thought would destroy me. But when it came to Liam, even when he'd been in over his head with the drugs, I'd never been in danger of losing myself. Liam brought out everything that was good inside of me. It was *without* him that I was on the edge of falling apart.

Clenching my jaw, I gathered my courage and turned in the direction of the OtherWorld buses. They had been touring all summer with three other bands, Demon's Wings co-headlining the tour with them. They had started the summer off with only two buses for their band, but I'd heard that they had added two more buses to their convoy since one member of OtherWorld had gotten married and another was recently engaged.

I didn't normally keep up with what was going on in the band unless it had something to do with Liam. But out of the blue, Emmie Armstrong had made a phone call to my manger, Annabelle, and offered me a nice-sized check to perform at Liam's little sister's wedding. I'd done the wedding but had refused the check.

Marissa Bryant—now Marissa Niall, I guess—was one of the few people I actually liked. She was the kind of person people were drawn to, whether they wanted to be or not. She'd been one of the few people to accept me without judgment.

Of course I'd used the chance to see Liam as well, but he hadn't let me get near him. Even at the reception, which I'd gone to in hopes of getting him to talk to me—even if for only five minutes, he'd basically hidden himself behind Emmie Armstrong at first and then Dallas Cage. I'd left feeling like a fucking stalker.

After that I'd been determined to put Liam Bryant out of my mind and out of my heart. I'd thrown myself into my music and, yeah, I'll admit it—one or two one-night stands. If Liam didn't want me then I wasn't going to continue to throw myself at him. I wasn't going to beg him to be with me.

Then I'd gotten the call from my aunt telling me that Nonno was sick and asking for me. I'd jumped on the first flight to Connecticut, torn apart that the man who had raised me might not make it through the night. The first words out of his mouth had shattered something inside of me and I'd sat in shocked silence as he'd confessed what he'd done that fateful New Year's Eve night.

Now, knowing what really happened and why Liam continued to push me out of his life, I couldn't let it continue. Not if there was even the slightest chance he still loved me. After what I'd found out, I was going to fight until my last breath was torn from my chest for the man who owned my soul.

I reached the buses and knocked on the first one that I came to. None of them were marked, or had the band's artwork on the side of them proclaiming they were OtherWorld. It was almost an Emmie Armstrong trademark to keep the buses as plain on the outside as possible. I understood it and was actually glad that Annabelle had the same mentality. When your life was front and center for the tabloids and social media, it was easier to breathe knowing that the public couldn't easily identify the vehicle you were basically living in while on tour. Anonymity was your lifeline out here on the road.

I didn't know if Liam had had time to get back to them or not, but it was as good a starting point as any. After a few moments the door opened and Marissa stood there looking down at me. The beautiful, voluptuous woman stared down at me with first a frown and then a small smile. "Hi, Brie."

At the sound of the nickname that Liam had originally given me, my heart clenched. Very few people had ever used that little nickname that I'd hated in the beginning. Now, even fewer people called me by it and it was a sweet kind of torture to my heart to hear it. "Hi, Rissa. Is he here?"

Marissa's face tightened for a moment and I could tell that she was fighting herself. I respected her for being so loyal to her brother, but that didn't mean I wasn't irritated that she didn't just give me a simple *yes* or *no*.

"He hasn't come back to the bus yet," Marissa finally told me. "He's been going for a run with Linc after the shows, to wind down. It helps with…everything."

I swallowed hard, nodding. I was thankful that Liam had found a new, healthier outlet for his addictions. I'd learned through a new, yet completely bizarre, ally that Liam was still holding strong with his recovery: going to meetings, staying away from temptations, and using exercise to fight cravings. So far the exercise had been the most helpful and I'd seen at the wedding exactly how healthy he was now.

Before, when Liam was still struggling—and losing—his battle with addiction, he had been more on the thin side. That hadn't deterred from his almost beautiful male perfection, however. I doubted anything ever would. But now, he was so much more devastating with at least thirty pounds of muscle added to him. His eyes were brighter, and his skin had a healthy glow.

I'd taken one look at him at Marissa and Wroth's wedding and had to fight my instant need for this new version of the man I loved. *Dio*, all I wanted was to be with him again.

"Do you know how long he will be?" I saw the hesitation on Marissa's lovely face and rushed to continue. "It's important that I speak to him, Rissa. Please…" I sucked in a deep breath and just spilled it all out. "My grandfather died last week, but before he passed he told me something that I had no clue about. Please, I need to talk to Liam."

Sympathy filled her eyes. "I'm so sorry about your grandfather."

I lowered my eyes. "Me too," I whispered. I hadn't really dealt with his being gone yet, not the way I knew I should have, not the way Alexis had. I was so determined to get Liam back as soon as possible that I hadn't let myself process that the man who had taken me in when my father had died, raised me—loved and protected me since I was ten years old—was actually gone.

I heard Marissa move and lifted my eyes quickly. She stepped down from the bus and took one of my hands, giving it a compassionate squeeze. "He won't be gone long, no more than an hour. As soon as he gets back I'll tell him you're looking for him. Okay?"

My teeth sank into my bottom lip to keep my chin from trembling. I didn't like to rely on other people when something this important was on the line, but I had to trust Marissa. If she told Liam and he decided I wasn't worth his time…

No, I wouldn't think negatively like that. I couldn't let the doubts cloud my mind when I was so close to getting him back. "I'll be at my bus."

She tightened her hold on my hand. "I'll make sure he comes over, Brie. I promise. But I can't promise things will go as you want them to. He's not the same person he was when you two were together. He's stronger, better…I won't say he's happier, but he is better." Her breath hitched as she blew out a small sigh. "All I want is for him to be happy."

I tried to give her a smile, but wasn't sure if my lips cooperated or not. "Me too, Rissa. Me too."

I took my time walking back to the bus. Even though all the other bands were done for the day, the crews were making sure things were in their right places, bands were still running on the adrenaline high that being on stage gave them, and groupies were running around doing what they always did. I dodged one person after another, my eyes not really taking any of it in as I mentally went through what I wanted to say to Liam. If he came to see me…

Someone bumped into me and I lifted my head, realizing I had ended up on the other side of the lot where all the buses were parked without even noticing. My own bus was in the opposite direction. Damn.

Checking my watch I realized that I really must have been in a daze because the hour Marissa had said Liam would be gone was almost up. Cursing under my breath, I turned toward my bus.

I don't know what originally caught my eyes. With the cooling of the night's summer temperatures I could understand why someone would be wearing a hoodie. It was the way they kept their head down that really caught my eye, quickly followed by the shock of long, auburn hair on the little girl that the hoodie-wearer had in their arms.

I stopped for a moment to process what I was seeing. Even in the dim lighting coming from the parking lot's street lamps, I knew who that little girl was. The beautiful alabaster skin, the long red-gold auburn hair, and the eyes I knew were green told me that it was Emmie Armstrong's little mini-me. Mia was my little nephew's best friend. I'd seen her at a few of the playdates she sometimes had with Jordan and knew that she was her mother's daughter in more ways than just looks. Mia was full of fire and spunk and even though she was the daughter of the one chick I hated most in the world, I still couldn't help but smile when I saw her and Jordan playing together.

The fire and spunk was not on that beautiful little face tonight, though. I saw tears running down her face; saw fear in that lovely, pale face. I glanced around, looking for any sign of her mother, but knew instinctively that I wasn't going to see Emmie. Demon's Wings were on stage and the sound of the crowd even from where I was standing told me that they were definitely having a great show.

When the person in the hoodie disappeared from my line of sight, every maternal instinct inside of me started screaming at me to follow. Without even thinking about it, I started after them. At first at just a quick walk, but when Hoodie started moving faster I started jogging.

"Mia?" I called after them, hoping that I was wrong and that the person carrying the little girl was just one of Emmie's staff. But they weren't heading toward the Demon's Wings buses—they had been close to OtherWorld's and I'd already passed them.

The sound of my voice had Hoodie stiffening and turning their head a second before they broke into an all-out run. Fear churned in my stomach and I pulled my phone from my pocket, but instinct told me I didn't have time to stop and call anyone. Hoodie was taking Mia, was most probably kidnapping her. I couldn't let them take her, couldn't let Emmie go through the worst nightmare a mother could ever face, whether I hated her or not. That didn't matter. All that did was getting Mia out of Hoodie's arms.

Hoodie left the parking lot and ran onto a street that was just outside the stadium the rock festival was being held at. The street was deserted and I was able to gain ground on them when Hoodie fell. My heart clenched, and I feared Mia was hurt from the fall.

When I saw Mia squirming free, I raced to lift her into my arms. "Mia, are you okay, sweetheart?"

"I-I w-want my m-m-momma," Mia sobbed brokenly against my chest.

I wanted to reassure her that I would take her straight back to her momma, but the words stuck in my throat when Hoodie got to her feet and stepped in front of me. This close I could easily tell that it was a woman, but the only thing I could see of her face was the birthmark on her chin.

"I don't think so, bitch. You aren't messing this up for me." She moved so fast I barely had time to think. I saw the glint of metal flashing in the dim lighting of the street lamp seconds before I realized what it was.

A gun.

I didn't know what to do, but my first instinct was to protect Mia. I shifted her in my arms, praying that she would be safe just as the sound of the gun going off filled the air.

My chest suddenly felt on fire. I tightened my hold on Mia as I looked down and saw the blood staining my T-shirt. The next shot that went off seemed to deafen me and my next breath tasted like the blood I knew was filling my lungs.

I tried to shift Mia so that when I fell I wouldn't hurt her, but knew that there was no getting past it. It was either take her with me, or let her go and risk Hoodie taking her again.

Fucking hell, that hurts like a bitch. That was my last thought as my knees buckled and the world started to go dark.

Liam

My heart was pounding more now than it had on the run I'd taken earlier with Linc.

Everything was on lockdown.

No one was allowed in or out of the stadium. Police had everyone detained until Mia Armstrong could be found. If she could be found. I'd barely stepped through the door when Marissa had barged onto my bus, but before she could even open her mouth Dallas had run in saying we had to find Mia.

Since then we had been divided into groups to search for the little girl. I'd gone with Dallas, Emmie, and the bodyguard named Peterson. I was terrified for the Emmie's little girl, shaking with reaction from the possibility that my friends could have lost their daughter forever. If I was taking it like this then I couldn't even imagine what Emmie and Nik must have been feeling.

I followed Emmie, checking the opposite side of the street but keeping up with her as much as I could while still looking everywhere a small little girl could hide or be hidden. Dallas, even while pregnant, was moving faster than any of us. She and Peterson were farther ahead and I was sure that it was to make sure Emmie didn't stumble onto something that would send her into a nervous breakdown.

"It's her!" Dallas called out.

Relief washed over me and I left the small alley I'd just been looking down. There had been a trashcan, and the smell of something rotting coming from the drain beside the dumpster. I'd been praying that I would find Mia even as I had prayed I wouldn't. The smell of death that had been coming from that drain had made bile churn in my stomach as thoughts of it being Mia had...

I saw Emmie and Mia first. Emmie was holding onto her daughter as if she were her lifeline. Her shoulders were shaking, whether from sobs or reaction, I couldn't tell from back where I was.

"T-that m-m-mean lady tried to t-take m-me, Momma," Mia wailed. "I-I'm s-s-sorry I-I was b-bad."

"Oh baby. It's okay. You're okay. Momma's got you now. No one is going to take you. Okay?"

"A-a-aunt Gabs s-s-saved me," she whispered brokenly. "H-help her, Momma. Help her."

Mia's plea for her mother to help "Aunt Gabs" hit me wrong. I didn't know how, but I just knew who "Aunt Gabs" was. I'd heard it so many times on the weekends when I was living with Gabriella that hearing it then, coming from that scared little baby's mouth, made everything inside of me freeze. Despite the horror of the past half hour or so, I suddenly felt as if I was in a dream as I looked past Emmie and Mia and turned my eyes on Dallas and Peterson for the first time.

They were on their knees on the broken concrete of the street, both doing CPR on the lifeless person lying on the ground. I had no idea if it was the person who had taken Mia or not, but that didn't seem to matter to my brain as I took a shaky step forward and saw her face for the first time.

No, my brain whispered. *No. God, please. No!*

Everything inside of me seemed to shut down for a minute. I couldn't breathe, couldn't think, couldn't fucking see anything but that pale, beautiful face that haunted my dreams.

"Brie!" Her name felt like it was being torn from my chest as the night air filled with my scream and I fell to my knees beside her. In less than a second, I took in everything that was really going on.

She was lying there, not breathing, and there was so much blood. So. Much. Blood. "What happened? Why is there so much blood?"

"Gunshot," Peterson bit out as he pressed down on her chest, continuing to give Gabriella life-saving CPR. "Two to the chest."

"Liam, focus." Dallas grabbed my hand when I reached out to touch Gabriella's face, snapping me out of the daze I was starting to fall into. "The paramedics are on their way, but this street is deserted. Go meet them."

I just sat there, my sweats soaking up the blood of the only person who could ever really hold my heart in her hand, not really understanding the words coming from my friend's mouth. There was blood smeared across her forehead, as if she'd used her bloody hand to brush hair out of her eyes. Her blue eyes were bright with some emotion I couldn't put a name to because I was numb to everything else but the pain ripping through my chest. Dallas tightened her hold on my hand. "Don't fall apart on me, Liam. Not now. Gabriella needs you. Every second counts. Go meet the paramedics, show them where we are. She has two bullets in her chest. They are still inside her, Liam. Do you understand? No exit wounds. She needs more help than I can give her right now."

That snapped me out of it and I was on my feet and running. Dallas was a nurse. She knew what she was talking about. If she said that Gabriella needed more help, then I was going to get it for her. As I ran I began to whisper a prayer, that whoever might have been watching over my Brie would protect her until I could get back to her.

The sound of sirens caught my attention and I saw the flashing lights as they quickly approached. I ran faster and started waving my arms to get their attention. The paramedics started to slow down but I didn't want to speak to them, didn't want them to waste so much as a nanosecond of time getting to my girl. Talking took up too much time, and time was not on Gabriella's side at the moment.

I turned and started running back the way I'd just come, running faster than I'd ever run in my life, glancing over my shoulder only once to make sure that the ambulance was right behind me. As soon as I reached them and saw that Peterson and Dallas had switched positions, with Dallas doing compressions and Peterson breathing air into Gabriella's mouth, I went straight back to my girl.

Dropping down next to her, I grabbed her hand and lifted it to my lips. Her fingers were cold, her hand lying limp in my tight grip. *Don't leave me. Please don't leave me.* This wasn't happening. It couldn't be. No way would God punish me like this. I had given Gabriella up, had pushed her as far as possible out of my life knowing that I was nothing but trouble for her. She deserved so much better than a junkie who would only bring her down. I'd given her up, made the greatest sacrifice I'd ever had to make in my entire life.

I'd only been able to survive this without her beside me because I knew she would be better off, but also because she was still out there. Somewhere. She still had her whole life in front of her, and as long as she was healthy and happy, then I could stay strong.

But if she weren't, if she were taken from this world and God didn't take me too…

Then life wasn't really worth it, was it?

The sound of Dallas shouting orders to the two paramedics had me dropping Gabriella's cold little hand and moving out of the way. I wasn't going to hinder anyone helping her, even if everything inside of me was screaming to hold onto her as tightly as possible.

A cool hand touched my arm and I jerked in surprise as I lifted my eyes to meet the wet, green eyes of Emmie Armstrong. She stood over me, holding a blood-soaked, still-sobbing Mia tightly against her. "I'm going to take Mia to Nik and then I will be right behind the ambulance. Stay strong, Liam. I'll take care of everything else. Just stay strong."

"Y-you will?" I muttered, confused. Why would Emmie help Gabriella? They hated each other. It wasn't just Emmie who hated Gabriella. My girl hated Emmie just as much, and it was my fault. I was the one who caused the initial feud between them. I'd lit the match that had sent them in opposing corners, ready to come out swinging the second the bell rang.

The question must have been in my eyes because she grimaced and held her daughter even tighter. "Because right now, I owe her everything. Not even my own life is enough to repay her for saving Mia."

Swallowing hard, I nodded at her explanation. Emmie turned away from the chaos that was going on around me, taking Mia back to the safety of her father's arms.

And I prayed harder.

The next ten minutes felt like they took a lifetime, yet were over in almost the blink of an eye. The medics and Dallas moved quickly, loading Gabriella up, putting in an IV, putting a manual oxygen mask over her face and squeezing air into her lungs while Dallas climbed onto the gurney with her to continue doing compressions that kept Gabriella's heart pumping.

I jumped into the front seat with the driver, and he didn't even give me a second glance as he turned his sirens back on and drove like the hounds of hell were chasing us toward the closest hospital. I had a sudden vision that we were racing something straight out of hell. We were racing Death, and he was hot on our heels after my girl. My *everything*.

When we reached the hospital, things moved even faster, but the vision of the man in the black cloak vanished from my mind and I was able to breathe just a little easier. The trauma team was already there, waiting and ready to take over, but Dallas never moved from her position on top of Gabriella even as they transferred her from one gurney to another and ran toward the elevators. I stood with Peterson as the doors shut behind them, stabbing my fingers through my hair, not caring that I was smearing blood everywhere.

"Where are they taking her?" I demanded of the first nurse I saw.

"She's being taken straight into surgery, sir. The patient has two bullets still inside of her somewhere. They are more dangerous inside than out." Her kind eyes drifted over me from head to toe, taking in my blood-stained clothes, the smears on my cheeks and forehead and the tears blinding my eyes. "Let me show you where you can get cleaned up."

"No," I growled. I didn't give a fuck about what I looked like. I just wanted to be somewhere closer to her. Damn it, I wanted to switch places with Gabriella, take the pain she was in. Fight death for her. Go to hell in her place if God would just take me instead. "No, just show me where I can wait."

She nodded and turned for the elevators, a different set than those that had just taken Gabriella away from me. Peterson followed, staying close, but I didn't really notice or care. Around me, the hospital was starting to turn into a circus freak show, with nurses stopping to stare and whisper as I passed. With all the scandals I'd caused in the past with my drug abuse and other bullshit, I was easily recognizable. Soon the reporters would be swarming the place and I would have no privacy, but right then and there none of that mattered.

All I wanted was for my Brie to live.

I couldn't sit down.

The OR waiting area wasn't overly crowded, although there were a few families spread out around the room. Anxiety was raging through me and I couldn't stand the thought of sitting. So I paced from one side of the room to the other. I didn't feel the eyes of the others following me, didn't see the flash of someone's smartphone as they snapped a few pictures.

I was blind to the outside world, instead trapped in my own personal hell. Question after question was tearing through my mind like a hot blade. *Why was Brie even at the rock festival?* I hadn't known she was going to be there until one of the roadies had mentioned that he'd seen her bus just before OtherWorld had taken the stage.

How had she found Mia?

Which left me wanting to find the motherfucker and tear them apart with my bare hands. I could do it. I had the strength, and with the mixed martial arts that Linc had been adding to our workouts lately, I could do it a lot more easily. My hands balled into fists as I fantasized about how I would destroy the person who might have taken my soul away from me.

Two cold, soft hands landed on my shoulders. I turned without thinking, ready to fight whoever had grabbed me, my fist raised at the ready. Dallas stood there, no fear in her tired blue eyes. I dropped my fists, forcing them to relax at my sides. I ran my gaze over the girl who was quite possibly my best friend in the world.

There were bloody finger smears all over her pale face. Her long blond hair was disheveled; most of her ponytail was down around her shoulders. Her clothes were even more blood-soaked than my own, gluing her shirt to her small baby-bump.

"H-how is she?" I whispered, unable to force my voice any louder. It wasn't the question I wanted to ask, but the only one I could bear to let leave my throat.

Dallas seemed to understand that. One blood-covered hand lifted and squeezed at her neck as she blew out a long, tired breath. "I don't know what to tell you at the moment, Liam. Things didn't look good when they forced me out of the operating room. They have to go in and find the bullets, which could be anywhere, and who knows what kind of damage they did in there. I'm sorry."

"What…" I stopped and cleared my throat. "What can I do?"

"Pray, Liam. That's all anyone can do right now."

Before I could process that, the waiting room door opened and it was like a tidal wave of craziness began. Emmie walked through the door, followed by some dude in a wrinkled suit, and three security guards. The guards and the guy in the suit went straight to the other families waiting and spoke quietly to each of them.

Within five minutes they were gone, moved to another waiting room on the other side of the same floor. Maybe I should have felt bad that those people had to be moved, but I couldn't spare so much as a second thought for them. I didn't give a fuck if those people had sick friends and family that they cared about and were waiting just as anxiously for news about like I was. They didn't matter, not to me.

The security guards were quickly replaced with big men in suits from Seller's security firm. I'd seen them all over the last few months, ever since the first attack on Shane and Harper's bus. Emmie had beefed up security for all of us, but not even that had protected Mia.

The hospital was put on high alert and the OR floor was basically put on lockdown. If you didn't need to be on this floor, then you weren't allowed onto it. It was a safety measure for not only Gabriella and probably anyone who was in the waiting room now, but also for the entire hospital. Fans, paps, and any other crazy could have gotten onto the floor to get the story of a lifetime or become the story. The guards would make sure that didn't happen.

Emmie sat in a chair by the window with her phone pressed to her ear. I spared her one long glance before I continued to pace. Her face was gray, new lines around her mouth and eyes making her look a few years older than she really was. If I was in hell right now, then she was right there with me. I wondered briefly how Mia was doing, what she'd seen tonight. Did she know who had done this to her? Had she seen who had shot Gabriella?

Before I could let the questions consume me, I turned my attention to Dallas who sat alone, rubbing her stomach and watching me. I'd heard parts of the conversation she'd had with Axton, telling him to stay at the bus with their son. She didn't want Cannon at the hospital and didn't want anyone but his father to watch him. I could understand that, since all the parents were probably going insane with the near miss with Mia tonight.

Peterson left at some point, but I didn't notice. He was Harper Stevenson's personal bodyguard and after the mess that someone had made of her and Shane's bus tonight, I figured he wanted to be closer to her. Marissa and Wroth arrived but didn't approach me, just took a seat beside Dallas.

Hours passed. My mind wouldn't slow down and I felt like I was going to go insane if I didn't hear some news soon. I'd given up on praying, had started begging and even negotiating. Asking God, the devil—fucking anyone who would listen to my silent pleas—to take me instead. I would gladly give up my life if it meant Gabriella would live.

She had so much to live for, so many people who needed her. Alexis, Jordan, her old bastard of a grandfather...

I groaned and leaned back against one of the walls. I closed my eyes and bent in half. She deserved to live. It should have been me in there, fighting that damn tug of war with Death. I was the fuckup; I was the ex-junkie who'd screwed up my life repeatedly. It should have been me. *God, please. Just...please. Take me.* "Fuck." It was the first word I'd spoken aloud in hours and even to my own ears it sounded broken and hoarse.

"Li?"

My eyes opened to find my sister crouched in front of me, tears in her eyes and her hulk of a husband right behind her. "Rissa," I murmured and felt my throat burn with yet more tears at the sight of hers. I must have cried a damn river tonight, but I still had more to shed. Rissa should never have to cry. Never. With each one that spilled from her pretty eyes I broke a little more.

Marissa's soft hands cupped my face, one thumb brushing away a stray tear. "What can I do for you, Li? How can I help?"

"I…" I cleared my throat and shook my head, trying to clear it. "Her cousin… Lee-Lee. She needs to know before she hears it on the news."

"Emmie already called her and her manager. Both are on their way," Marissa assured me. "The manager was just a few hours away, and Alexis is already on a plane. It's okay, Li. Emmie is taking care of all of it. Just concentrate on Gabriella…and you."

Across the room the door opened again and my stomach churned, hoping it was the doctor, praying it wasn't if there wasn't going to be good news. But it wasn't a doctor who walked into the room to tell me if my reason for living was okay or not.

No, it was a blast from the past in the shape of long platinum-blond hair with hot-pink streaks, a curvy body that had once been anything but, and the same attitude that had once made me laugh. My eyes widened and I straightened.

"Annabelle?" Wroth spoke for the first time, apparently just as surprised as I was to see the chick standing there.

I hadn't seen her in seventeen years, but I would know her anywhere. The girl who had lived between Devlin and Zander when we were growing up. The sister of our original lead singer before he'd decided he didn't want to be in a rock band but wanted a wife and country music instead.

When OtherWorld had gotten the contract with Rich Branson, we'd moved on and I hadn't seen either her or Noah since. Although I did know that Noah had made a name for himself in the country music world and I had seen a few stories on him and his family in the tabloids from time to time, no one had heard from Noah or even Annabelle since…

Annabelle Cassidy stepped farther into the room, her eyes taking in the room-at-large before stopping on me. "Is there any news?"

Liam

My shock at seeing Annabelle was short lived as the door behind her opened and in walked a man in sweaty, green scrubs. He was a few inches shorter than me, with a wrinkled face and balding gray head. The look in his eyes was tired, but determined.

Determined was good, right?

Please, God. Let it be good.

"I'm Dr. Schiller and I'm going to assume that everyone in this room is here for Gabriella Moreitti." His voice was low and rough, but I heard him clearly.

Stepping forward, I offered him my trembling hand. "I'm her fiancé," I rushed to tell him. No way was I going to tell this dude that I was her ex-boyfriend and that I hadn't spoken to her in over a year. He would probably have the security guards toss my ass out of the hospital. When he shook my hand, I asked the one question I needed the answer to: "How is she?" *Please be alive. Please don't let her have left me.*

The doctor motioned toward one of the many empty chairs around the room. "Let's have a seat." He sat down in a chair close to Dallas and I took the seat beside him even though I wasn't sure if I would remain sitting for long.

Everyone else took a seat close to us, watching and listening intently. Even Emmie had put her phone away and had her eyes trained on the doctor. "How is she?" I repeated.

"She's stable but still in critical condition." He leaned back in the chair, looking exhausted, and my fear started to choke me. He started talking in doctor lingo and I was lost before he even really began.

I looked past the doctor to Dallas, silently begging her to explain to me what the fuck the doctor was really saying. She scrubbed her blood-stained hands over her face and blew out a long breath. "The bullets ricocheted around inside of her, Liam. It caused a lot of damage. Hit several important organs. He's stopped the internal bleeding it's caused, but her lungs got the worst deal. He's giving her a fifty-fifty chance of making it through the night. If she does, the odds will go up tomorrow in her favor, but not by much. What he's really saying is that the next forty-eight to seventy-two hours are going to be long ones."

I knew she wouldn't sugarcoat the truth, but the reality of what she was saying made my stomach clench and I was pretty sure I'd stopped breathing. The world started to blur, bile rose in the back of my throat. No, I wasn't going to accept that. I couldn't. If God took Gabriella, if he took my Brie from this world, then I would follow her. I would be right behind her.

Two strong hands landed on my shoulders and Wroth's hulk-like form was suddenly right in front of me. "Take a deep breath, brother." His naturally growly voice replaced the buzzing in my ears and I forced myself to draw a breath.

This wasn't happening. I couldn't have a panic attack right now. Gabriella needed me to stay strong, not fall apart like a goddamn pussy. But it was hard to separate the emotions churning inside of me when all I wanted to do was cry like a fucking baby.

Times like this, when life got hard and I didn't know what to do—when I had no control over anything—was when I used to fall back on the drugs. When I could escape into the numbing fog that they could offer me and I could control the outcome of what was going on inside of me with how much poison I put into my body. I hadn't touched them since the night Gabriella had thrown me out of her life. I'd cleaned up my act, gone to rehab and actually taken it seriously for the first time with Dallas's help, and stayed clean this time.

The drugs would have been welcome, would have helped so fucking much right in that moment...

I pushed Wroth back and he went, not because I could actually move him, but because he was willing to go. Turning back to the doctor, I asked the second most important question that needed an answer: "Can I see her?"

Dr. Schiller stood. "We've moved her into ICU. If you want to follow me, I'll take you in to see her. But I can only offer you a few minutes, son."

"I'll take anything you give me," I assured him and stood quickly to follow him.

Behind me I heard Marissa speaking to Wroth. "This is a nightmare. If feels just like when Li had the accident."

I nearly stumbled as I stepped through the waiting room door. Was this really what that had been like for them? Had they gone through this hell, felt this rollercoaster ride of emotions as they waited for me to wake up after I'd been in the wreck?

Had Gabriella felt what I'm feeling now as she'd sat beside me in ICU?

Fuck, I hoped not. I wouldn't wish this nightmare on anyone, but especially not my sister or Gabriella.

I kept pace with the doctor. He opened the door to the ICU ward and stepped inside. The place was quiet except for the annoying sounds of heart monitors *beep-beep-beeping*. I had tunnel vision as he walked past a nurses' station and then waited as a sliding glass door opened and he stepped inside. I saw nothing but the back of the old doctor's balding head as he moved forward and stopped beside the hospital bed.

Then, and only then, did I shift my eyes to the girl lying so still on that small bed. My breath suddenly felt trapped in my lungs. I stood there, frozen with a fear that clutched at my heart and seemed to stab its dagger-like fingernails through the middle of that stupid, weak organ.

There were tubes and wires and so many machines hooked up to her. IVs in her arm, putting both fluids and blood back into her and a chest tube sticking out of both her sides. There was a tube down her throat, sticking out of her mouth and attached to a machine that was breathing for her. Monitors were making noises that terrified me. Her long, dark hair was in tangles across her pillow and her once vibrant, olive complexion was now pale and lifeless. My heart rate slowed until it was matching the weak *beep-beep-beeping* coming from her heart monitor, as if it only wanted to mimic hers.

Should it stop, then so would mine.

Tears blurred my eyes, making it hard to see my little Italian rock goddess. I took a step closer on legs that threatened to buckle, they were shaking so badly. The pain that I almost always felt in the leg that had the rod didn't even register as I moved toward Gabriella. "C-can I touch her?" I asked the doctor but wasn't sure if he heard me or not because I had barely whispered the question.

"Of course. It might even help." He pushed the only chair in the room close to the right side of Gabriella's bed. "Sit, hold her hand and talk to her. Let the girl know that you are here and give her a reason to fight. Right now, her life is in God's hands, but she needs to fight for it, too."

I dropped into the chair and reached out, grasping hold of one cold hand. Mine weren't much warmer, but I rubbed my fingers over hers, offering all the warmth I could give. The *beep-beep-beeping* increased for a split second before falling back into its weak rhythm.

"I'll give you a few minutes alone," Dr. Schiller muttered and I heard the sliding glass door open and close behind him.

I didn't bother to turn to see if he was gone. It didn't matter who heard what I said to her as long as I spoke the words. "Don't leave me, Brie. Don't you fucking dare, baby. If you leave, then expect me right behind you. I can't...I won't live without you in this world. Do you hear me?" I lowered my head and pressed my trembling lips to the back of her icy hand. "Don't go, baby. P—" I broke off when my voice cracked and took a moment to get myself under control before I started sobbing like a baby. "Please don't go."

Chapter Three

Gabriella

I felt like I was floating, that my mind wasn't even a part of my body. I could hear noises but they sounded so far away and echoed a little, as if they were coming from a deep cave or something. I felt no pain, no emotion as I floated.

It was almost kind of peaceful. Almost.

Through the background noises, one stood out more than any other. A voice. *His* voice. Liam. I struggled to listen, to hear what he was saying, but only caught a few of his words. "…Leave me, Brie. You can't… Love…me…Go... Baby, please."

The dreamlike peacefulness started to vanish and my heart twisted painfully. What was he saying? He wanted me to leave him? He didn't love me? I didn't understand, refused to believe he wanted me to leave him. Where would I go? How would I fucking survive if he didn't want me, didn't love me?

Other noises, more annoying noises, started to drown out the precious sound of his voice. A loud *beep-beep-beeping* that sounded just like a garbage truck warning as it backed up. It made a weird kind of sense to my fogged-up mind. He was telling me to go, throwing my love back at me like the garbage it must have been to him.

I struggled to breathe through my pain, tried to push it down. *Think of something else, Gabriella. Hurry before this pain consumes you. Think of something else.*

With a silent moan I turned it all off, and forced my mind onto something else. The sounds faded until I couldn't even hear Liam's voice, but that made my chest hurt even worse and I tried to imagine a happier time. A time when I didn't wonder if Liam loved me, if he wanted to be with me.

Instead I went straight back to the beginning, back to when I had first met Liam Bryant and OtherWorld. It wasn't peaceful, but at least it made the pain in my chest manageable.

Seven Years Earlier

For a girl who grew up playing Chopin but dreamed of playing Metallica, getting to tour with not one but two of the hottest rock bands in the world at the moment was a dream come true. I'd spent the majority of my life learning under some of the greatest teachers at Julliard, but not once had I let myself imagine that I would one day get to do what I'd secretly hoped for.

Yet here I was, with my band and our own tour bus, getting ready to tour Europe and then Australia for the next six months as the opening act for OtherWorld and Demon's Wings.

Our plane had touched down late the night before and we'd been shuttled to the hotel at an ungodly hour. My band, all guys that I'd met at Julliard and who had the same dream as me to take our classical music and turn it into the next amazing rock sound, were all jet-lagged but I'd been full of energy and couldn't even think of sleeping.

OtherWorld and Demon's Wings were flying over from Miami, which had been their last stop before starting the European tour. I wasn't sure how my manager had pulled it off, getting me and the guys on the lineup for the tour, but I was going to give him the biggest fucking kiss the next time I saw him. Craig wasn't with us, but he'd assured me that if I needed anything, to call him or go straight to Emmie Jameson, the girl who basically ran point for Demon's Wings.

I'd never met the chick, but I'd heard a lot about her. Who hadn't? Even at twenty she was a big deal in the rock world. People wanted to sign with Rich Branson in hopes that Emmie Jameson would take them on and work her magic for them like she did for the Demons.

It was nearly dawn and the buses were about to arrive at any minute to get us loaded up. I had taken a shower and then ordered some room service when I got to my room. I wasn't tired so there wasn't any use in trying to get any sleep. Zipping up my carry-on, I lifted off my bed and headed for the door. I knocked on my drummer's door, just to make sure that he was awake before heading for the elevators.

Downstairs things were in complete chaos. I saw people loading up buses that had each band's artwork on them. Five of them in all, with two for the road crew and one each for the bands. They were smaller than what I would have imagined tour buses to be. Maybe it was a European thing, because the few buses I'd seen back in the States were massive compared to any of these buses.

With everyone running around, scrambling to do their jobs, one person stood out to me as I looked around. A small redhead with the most amazing alabaster skin, and even in the dim predawn light I could tell her big eyes were green. She had a clipboard in one hand and a cell in the other as she typed something one-handed into the smartphone while shouting out orders to people who passed her. This had to be Emmie Jameson.

I debated about whether or not to approach her and introduce myself. I started to take a step in her direction when someone stopped beside her and slung an arm around her small shoulders. My eyes widened when I recognized Axton Cage.

Holy shit! He's even hotter in person.

That thought had barely filled my mind when I saw Emmie drop the hand holding the phone and smiled up at the man the world had dubbed a rock god. His face changed when she smiled at him, becoming almost soft, and I wondered if they were together. It wouldn't have surprised me, but I had read an article just a few weeks before that said how sheltered the Demon's Wings right hand was by the band. With the reputation that Axton Cage had, I was sure that the Demons wouldn't let her get involved with the rocker if that were the case.

Mentally shrugging, I picked up my carry-on and turned toward the bus that had been decorated with the tour's logo, figuring that was my bus since the other two were more specific to the other bands. I hadn't taken more than half a step when I walked right into a wall of maleness.

Yelping, I stumbled back and landed on my ass. Muttering a curse, I glared up at the person who had let me fall on my rear. Long legs, lean waist. Not overly tall, but definitely not short. Shoulders that were lean, but hinted at a strength that suddenly had my panties dampening. Upward my eyes continued to travel until I got to his face.

Embarrassingly my mouth actually dropped open and I gaped up at the most beautiful man I'd ever laid eyes on. Never, not even once, had I considered a man to be beautiful, but this one? There just weren't any other words for him.

Liam Bryant.

And he was laughing at me.

"Hello there, beautiful." He chuckled as he crouched down in front of me and folded his arms over his knees. Blue eyes shined brightly down at me in a way that I suspected wasn't only because of his amusement at my expense. Given his reputation, it could have been the drugs he was on, or might have been some of the same instant desire that I was feeling right then and there. Maybe both.

Blowing out an embarrassed sigh, I pushed my hair out of my eyes and offered him my hand. "Don't just stand there, jackass. Help a girl up."

"Sexy. I like that slight Italian accent. Does it get thicker when you get pissed...or when a man's between your legs?" I instantly felt my cheeks fill with heat, not only because I was a little embarrassed but also because I could picture him between my legs, making me cry out in Italian as he gave me one orgasm after another.

His grin grew bigger and he pretended to hesitate a moment before finally taking my hand. As soon as his fingers wrapped around mine, I had a sudden urge to jerk them back. The heat of his hand felt like it was scalding my palm, sending electrical currents up my arm and zapping something in my chest. My heart rate increased as he pulled me to my feet and then roughly against him.

"Easy there, little Brie."

My eyes narrowed on him as I met his gaze. "Excuse me?"

"You're Gabriella Moreitti, right? I like 'Brie' better," he murmured in a voice deep with what I could only describe as sexual promises. "Yeah, Brie definitely fits you better, baby. A small, beautiful name for my little goddess."

Everything inside of me felt like it had touched a white-hot flame. I felt my body tremble as he pushed against me, ever so slightly. There was no mistaking the hardness pressed against my stomach. He wanted me just as much as I wanted him. Holy hell, I'd never felt attraction so strong in my entire life. The lovers I'd had in the past had never been able to get me this hot—*this wet*—so quickly. And he hadn't even really touched me.

Yet, a small voice whispered suggestively in the back of my mind.

Swallowing a moan, I shifted my eyes to his lips. I wondered what he tasted like. Would his lips be sweet or spicy? I wanted to discover the answer so damn badly.

I'd never been one to think with my pussy. I liked to think I was smarter than that. Yet, in that moment, I was willing to let it take over and my brain wasn't really giving me any reason not to dive into discovering how good of a lover the rocker holding me against him actually was.

I tore my eyes from his lips and met his gaze full on, boldly letting him see that I was up for whatever ride he was willing to take me on. Those blue eyes darkened to cobalt and the grin disappeared. "You're a dangerous one, Brie." He released his hold on me and stepped back. "I'll have to remember that," he called over his shoulder as he turned and left me standing there.

All the heat that had been burning me alive just a moment ago turned into ashes and I felt instantly cold as I watched him walk away. *What the fuck was that?* I'd pretty much just offered myself up to him and he'd walked away from me. Had the last few minutes been a game to him? Every ounce of desire I'd just been feeling turned into anger and I picked up my carry-on and stomped onto my bus.

Three of my five bandmates were already on there, sorting our things out. Martin, my bass player, gave me a smile as I stepped into what was considered the living room. I knew he had a thing for me, but there was no way I was hooking up with him. The guy was a pig, but he was one hell of a bassist. I pushed past him and down the hall to the roosts where I threw my bag onto the first bed I came to and fell onto the mattress.

Fuck Liam Bryant anyway.

I stayed there for over half an hour before I heard a female voice coming from the front of the bus. Muttering a curse under my breath, I stood and went back into the small living room. Emmie Jameson was standing by the door with her clipboard in one hand and Jesse Thornton standing behind her like a bald, warrior angel.

His eyes changed from one shade of brown to another so quickly I was caught off guard for a moment. The sound of Emmie asking a question that was directed at me pulled me out of my curious daze and I met her green gaze.

"I'm sorry, what did you say?" Damn it, I wasn't normally so spaced out. I blamed Liam Bryant. He'd done something to warp my brain.

"I was asking if you needed anything," she said with a small, exasperated sigh. "I'm not used to touring with a female lead, so if you have any problems with anyone, be sure and let me know. I don't put up with anyone disrespecting the chicks I'm responsible for."

I crossed my arms over my chest, a little miffed that she thought she had to be responsible for me. "Thanks for the offer, but I can take care of myself." I'd been dealing with dickhead musicians most of my life. I could handle anyone who tried to fuck with me.

Emmie's lips lifted in a *yeah right* kind of smile, but she didn't say another word about it. I wanted to tell her that she didn't need to worry about me, that not only did I have self-defense training but I also carried pepper spray with me everywhere I went. I didn't because she didn't seem like she would have cared one way or another. I shrugged and took a seat on the sofa as she ran down a list of dates, scheduled stops, and what was going to happen in between.

When she left, the buses started up and soon we were on the road. I sat in the living room with my band for a few hours but couldn't force myself to concentrate on the conversations going on around me. All I could think about was how affected I'd been by Liam Bryant. How affected I still was.

And how hurt I was that he'd turned his back on me after I'd basically thrown myself at him.

The asshole.

Liam

I was holding her hand so tight that at first I didn't realize she was moving her fingers. When they flexed in my hold, my heart leaped, and I lifted my eyes to her face, hoping she would have those beautiful brown eyes open for me.

They were still closed, her eyes moving rapidly behind the closed lids. I stood and leaned over her. "Brie, I'm here. Come back to me, baby. Please. I love you so damn much. Come on, look at me."

The movement stopped just as suddenly as it had begun and the monitor on the other side of her bed made a noise that had my heart stopping. Bells started ringing in warning and that *beep-beep-beeping* I'd found a little annoying when I'd first come in disappeared.

"No," I cried and tightened my hold on her hand. "Don't do this. Come back. I need you, Brie. I fucking need you."

The glass door behind me opened, and the room was filled with nurses and doctors. "Code Blue!" the doctor shouted before snapping out orders. I knew I was in the way, but I couldn't find the strength to let her go. If I released her hand I might never get the chance to hold it again.

Someone pushed me out of the way. "Sir, you need to wait in the waiting room."

"No!" I pushed against the nurse's hold. "She needs me. Fuck, *I* need her. Please," I begged, forcing back a sob. "Please, I can't leave her."

"She's in cardiac arrest, sir. There is nothing you can do but get in our way. You have to wait outside or I'll be forced to have security remove you." Her grip on my arms tightened and she gave me a firm shake, surprising me with her strength enough to pull my eyes from the scene that I knew was going to haunt my dreams for the rest of my life. My little Italian goddess looked so small and fragile on that hospital bed. Pale. *Lifeless.* "I can see that you care about her, sir. But if you want to give her a chance to ever open her eyes again, you have to let us do our job."

"Clear!" Dr. Schiller yelled before I heard the sound of defibrillator paddles being pressed to Gabriella's chest. The zapping sound filled my ears, and my eyes were glued to the small body on the hospital bed. Bile rose in the back of my throat as the doctor pressed the defibrillator to her chest again. She jerked as if she'd been electrocuted, but the sweetest noise reached my ears and I fell to my knees in front of the nurse still holding onto my arms, tears pouring down my face.

"She's back," Dr. Schiller announced. "Let's get her back into surgery. I must have missed something."

Two pairs of stronger arms jerked me to my feet and guided me out of the ICU as the medical team rushed Gabriella out of the room and down a different hall than I was pushed in. A door opened and I was suddenly standing in front of Dallas, Marissa, and Alexis Moreitti.

"What happened?" I thought I heard Emmie demanding of the two security guards still holding onto my arms.

"Miss Moreitti went into cardiac arrest. Her heart stopped but the doctor was able to bring her back. She's been taken back into surgery," the nurse who had tried to get me out of Gabriella's room explained, but I didn't look at her.

My eyes were trained on Alexis, Gabriella's best friend and the only person she really trusted in the world. She had a cane in one hand, still needing that small assistance to move around after the car accident that had nearly taken her life all those years ago. At the nurse's explanation, her face paled even more than it already was and her eyes filled with tears.

I had expected her to start cursing at me, to hit me. Anything. I would have welcomed it. She'd never really liked me and I couldn't really blame her. Instead she began to sway and I jerked away from the security guards still holding onto my arms. As those brown eyes so like her cousin's began to close, I caught her against my chest.

Lifting her into my arms, I carried her to the closest chair and sat down with her in my lap. I might not have been able to do anything for Gabriella right then, but if I didn't help Alexis, Gabriella would be pissed. I held her against me, carefully stroking her long, dark hair back from her delicate face. To look at this beautiful woman you would never really understand how strong she was. On the outside she looked so fragile, so easily broken.

Like her beloved cousin, Alexis wasn't. She was one of the strongest chicks I'd ever met. It had taken guts and an inner strength that few people possessed to survive the things she had fought through—and still continued to fight with every day of her life.

Annabelle produced a wet paper towel and pressed it against Alexis's forehead. The nurse who had come with me from the ICU ward waved something under the woman's nose and Alexis groaned before opening her eyes. Instantly, tears filled her eyes and spilled down her cheeks.

"Liam," she sobbed brokenly and buried her face in my chest. "She has to be okay. S-she has to."

I pressed my trembling lips to her forehead and tucked her closer. "I know, Lee-Lee. I know."

Time passed slowly. Dawn came and so did more of Seller's security team. The events from the night before had officially hit national news, and now the entire hospital, not just the ICU floor, was on lockdown.

I sat in a chair next to Alexis and held onto her hand. I wasn't sure who was holding on the tightest, her or me. I didn't care. All I knew was that if I let go of Alexis then it was like I was letting go of Gabriella. She must have felt the same way, because if I so much as shifted in my seat, her hand would clench at mine harder.

We were each other's last connection to her.

A nurse came in every hour to let us know that Gabriella was still in surgery and gave us an update on their progress. She'd been shot twice with a .22 and the bullets had not only bounced around inside of her, but also fragmented. One of the fragments was still in there, causing unknown trouble. They had pinpointed where it was, but because of the size of it and the location they had to be extremely careful. Which was what was taking hour upon hour of nerve-racking time to finish.

The sun was fully up when Devlin, Natalie, Linc, and Zander walked through the ICU waiting room door. I didn't notice anything until I heard Annabelle's vehement curse.

"Motherfucking sonofabitch. Cock-sucking dickhead." I lifted my eyes from the tiled floor to see the cute little blonde glaring at Zander as he stood in front of her with wide, amazed eyes. "Seventeen years, you asshole. It's been seventeen years with not so much as a phone call and all you can say is 'looking good, babe'?" She stepped into his personal space and stood on tiptoes to get in his face, seething with an anger I didn't understand. "Fuck you, Zander Brockman. Fuck. You."

Annabelle turned and practically ran from the room, leaving a stunned Zander standing there with a pained look on his face. I glanced at my other two bandmates who shook their heads at me. Obviously they didn't know what that had been about any more than I did.

"You people sure know how to keep things interesting," a new, deep voice grumbled as Jared Moreitti stepped into the room.

Alexis released my hand and was across the room faster than anyone would ever think possible. Her husband wrapped her tightly in his arms and held her tenderly against him as she began to cry again. She clutched at his shirt, holding on for dear life while he whispered softly in her ear.

I leaned back in my chair, scrubbing my hands over my tired face. Natalie, who had been having a whispered conversation with Emmie since she had arrived, sat down beside me. Even the sight of her tiny baby-bump peeking out of her shirt didn't have the power to distract me as she patted me on the shoulder. "How are you hanging on?"

I shook my head. "I'm not, Nat. I'm slowly losing my mind."

Linc crouched down in front of me. "You need to go for a run or something, man. You're getting twitchy."

I glared at the man who had become one of my best friends in the world. Without his help I might have fallen back on the drugs a long time ago. But he stayed on my ass, making sure that I worked out every day and was always around in case I needed to talk when old cravings started fucking with my mind.

Right now I might have gone looking to score something to numb my mind if it weren't for one thing: I wasn't going to leave this hospital, this damn waiting room. Fuck the drugs. I didn't need them—even if I did crave them at that moment worse than I'd ever craved them. All I wanted—*all I fucking needed*—was for Gabriella to be okay.

"I'll be fine. I'm not going anywhere," I told him.

Devlin dropped down in the chair on the other side of me. It didn't surprise me that he was there. We'd put our past behind us after my accident more than a year ago. Why should I hold what had happened with Tawny against him when that bitch hadn't really meant anything to me? Maybe we weren't as tight as we had been when we were teenagers, but we were close enough to make me glad that he was there now. "You look thirsty. How about some coffee?"

"No."

"I can order you something to eat?" Natalie offered. "Anything you want, just say the word."

I shook my head. "No, I'm not hungry." She opened her mouth, probably to offer me something else, but I cut her off. "Thanks for being here, sweetheart, but I don't want or need anything except for Brie to be okay. Unless you can make that happen, then please, just stop."

Natalie's chin trembled for a moment and I felt bad for making her cry, but before I could apologize she forced a smile for my benefit and leaned her head against my shoulder. "I'll just sit here and hold your hand. Okay?"

"Yeah, okay." I cleared my throat. "Thanks," I whispered.

They were all quiet for a long while, sitting with me and offering me the only thing I could accept right then.

Their love for me.

Chapter Five

Gabriella

That stupid tunnel thing was getting really fucking annoying.

I was tired of hearing noises but not really hearing them. Nothing made sense and it was seriously giving me a headache. Why couldn't I make out even so much as one word? I knew people were talking, but I couldn't understand the words or identify the voices. And even more annoying was that damn *beep-beep-beeping* sound that was once again driving me crazy.

I wanted to yell at someone to make it all stop, to just let me sleep, but I couldn't find the energy to open my eyes to see who was standing over me.

At least that floating feeling was gone. That had been a little scary and I was glad that I felt like I was back in my own body. Liam was gone, though, that much I did know. If it meant that he was still with me I would have gladly gone through that scariness forever.

It wasn't always like that, though. There was a time I would have pushed him out a window to get away from him. A few times during that first tour through Europe and then Australia I'd been tempted to do just that. The drugs had made him a real douchebag at times…

SEVEN YEARS EARLIER

Have you ever felt like you could conquer the world?

That was the way it felt when I was out on stage, whether it was performing some classical piece for an audience of two hundred or with my band rocking out with thirty-thousand fans. It was exhilarating—a natural high that kept me stoked for hours afterward.

We were five weeks into the three-month European tour. I was having the time of my life, and so were my bandmates. Opening for OtherWorld and Demon's Wings was no easy feat. Having to be the ones that got the crowd riled up for the real reason they were there was a definite challenge. It was one that I was determined to accomplish every night we stepped out on stage.

Tonight we had definitely succeeded. When OtherWorld was ready to take the stage, they were chanting my name, begging for one more song. Considering that the fans were there to see OtherWorld, not me and my band, that had been a thrill in itself.

By the end of the entire concert I was still flying high on the exhilaration and ready to go out partying with everyone else. A party bus was waiting for us all outside the back parking lot where our tour buses were parked. I'd taken my time getting ready so I was one of the last to climb on.

It was a madhouse inside the party bus. There were three stripper poles with talented chicks working them, with more strippers already giving some of the guys lap dances. I didn't know why we were going to a club when we had our own club right here. Booze was flowing freely and the noise was almost enough to rival that of the crowd earlier. It looked like fun and I was so ready for some fun.

Someone handed me a beer and a shot glass full of tequila. I downed the tequila and chased it with my beer as the bus started moving. Martin, my bassist, and Doug, who was my drummer, were sitting closer to the back of the bus with Jesse Thornton, Shane Stevenson, and Wroth Niall. Martin called out for me to come back and join them, and since I didn't have a better option I slowly made my way back there.

When one of the strippers on the second pole kicked her legs out into an upside down split, I was momentarily halted. Glancing down at who I'd been stopped in front of, I found myself staring into a pair of blue eyes that had been haunting my dreams for the last five weeks.

Liam Bryant was lounged back with one stripper practically sitting on his lap. He had a beer bottle in one hand and a bottle of absinthe in the other. From the look on his face, he was half out of his mind already, and the way the stripper was all over him I knew that at least one rocker was going to be having sex on this bus tonight.

Jealousy churned in my stomach but I met his gaze boldly, trying to show him that I didn't care what he did. No way was I going to let him know that I was still affected by him walking away from me that first day.

The stripper, a beautiful French chick, shifted enough that I could finally get by and I started to pass her. One jean-clad leg shot out and a booted foot bumped into my thigh with just enough force to send me toppling over into someone's lap, dropping my beer along the way.

I shot a glare at Liam, who'd kicked me. He gave me a smirk and went back to letting his stripper press her very fake tits into his face. Muttering a curse under my breath, I looked up at the guy who'd caught me and nearly groaned.

Axton Cage was grinning down at me. "Wow. This is a surprise, and it's not even my birthday. Lucky me."

I pushed against his chest, unable to mistake the smell of good whiskey on his breath. He was just as drunk as everyone else on the bus. His arms tightened on me when I tried to get up. "Let go," I snarled.

"Make me." Axton's hold on my waist tightened even more and he lifted me easily so that I was practically straddling his lap.

For a split second I thought about staying there. I'd discovered over the last five weeks that Axton Cage wasn't all that bad of a guy. He flirted a lot, drank just as much, and was always mooning over Emmie Jameson when he thought no one else was looking. I kind of felt sorry for him. Kind of. It might have been fun to just get lost in this rock god for a few hours.

From the back of the bus, Martin called my name again and I snapped out of my musings. Axton Cage might be fun for a few hours, but he wasn't the rocker I wanted to have fun with. Stupidly, I still wanted to be with Liam.

Fuck, I was such a masochist.

"Let her go, Ax," I heard come from the chick sitting beside Axton, and I turned my eyes on Emmie Jameson. She was sitting tucked between the rock god and Nik Armstrong. She was drinking a beer and looked bored to death. "She's not up for happy time with you tonight."

Axton's bottom lip pouted out, but his hold on me slackened. I got to my feet, nodded my thanks to Emmie, and went back to join my bandmates. Doug handed me another beer and I took the free space between him and the Demon's Wings drummer.

It was safer beside Doug than it was Martin. I didn't want to give him so much as the tiniest hint that I was interested. I wasn't and never would be. That didn't seem to matter to him. The guy was starting to skeeve me out. As soon as we got back to the States I was definitely going to find a replacement for him.

Doug tucked me against his side as he continued whatever conversation he'd been having with the two Demons and the lead guitarist for OtherWorld. Soon I was being pulled into it and laughing my ass off. Someone kept pushing a drink into my hands and I downed each one of them. By the time we reached the club, I was more than a little tipsy.

Things were crazy in the club. Most of the guys got lost in the crowd. I stuck close to Doug, Jesse, and Wroth for most of the night because they seemed more interested in getting drunk and talking than finding pussy. After my fifth shot and third beer though, they started to bore me and I escaped to the dance floor.

It didn't matter that I didn't have anyone to dance with. No one was really dancing with any one person anyway. I got lost in the beat of the music and before I knew it I was surrounded by strangers who were all having as much fun as I was.

When I finally left the dance floor, I was covered in sweat and dying of thirst. I pushed my way through the crowd to the bar and ordered two bottles of water. When the bartender handed them over I swallowed the contents of one without stopping for air. My throat was aching from a mixture of dehydration and exhaust from singing two nights in a row.

The schedule for this tour was off-the-walls crazy, since we were in a different city almost every other night. I wasn't going to complain, though. I was having the time of my life. The only thing that could have made this all better was if my cousin Alexis were there with me. I wished she were there instead of back in Connecticut dealing with a broken heart. If I ever saw Jared Giordano again I was going to kick his ass.

Taking my time drinking the second bottle of water, I turned around to people-watch. The first thing to catch my eye was the two idiots hanging from one of the light fixtures. And by two idiots I meant Martin and Zander Brockman. They were drunk off their asses and using the light fixtures as monkey bars.

If I'd been a little more sober I might have been concerned for them, but I wasn't. Their stupidity fascinated me as I watched Zander make it halfway across the room before Emmie finally noticed him and yelled at him to get down. While half the club watched the exhibition the two men were making, Zander looked down at her and shook his head. When she put her hands on her hips, looking more like a displeased mother than a twenty-year-old rock band assistant, his face paled a little and he jumped down onto the table he was hanging above.

Martin ignored her when she turned that displeased look on him and kept going. *Fall. Fall. Fall,* I mentally chanted. My inebriated state even wanted him to break something non-life threatening when he did.

He didn't.

A set of inked-up arms wrapped around Martin's legs and pulled him down. Martin landed on his back on a table, and I could tell he was laughing. Had the fucktard been getting into Liam's absinthe? I'd never seen him act so stupid in my life.

With the show over, most of the onlookers had gone back to what they'd been doing. I watched for a little longer, hiding a grin behind my bottle of water as I watched Emmie stand over Martin with a fuming Jesse Thornton right beside her. She was obviously ripping him a new one from the expression on Martin's face.

I seriously hoped the little redhead made him cry. I'd heard a few stories that she could do that with a look if she was pissed enough.

Jesse shifted when Emmie turned to speak to him and the rocker on the sofa behind the huge drummer immediately caught my attention. All the alcohol I'd swallowed earlier churned in my stomach as I watched Liam making out with some long-legged blonde chick. She wasn't one of the strippers from the party bus, but I'd seen Liam dancing with her earlier.

Now she was straddling his lap, her shirt pulled up over her bra while he filled his hands up with her impressive chest. Even from where I was standing across the room, I could see that she had her tongue down his throat. Neither of them seemed to care that they were pretty much having sex in the middle of a French nightclub. From the amount of absinthe Liam had drunk on the bus, I was sure that he didn't even remember where he was.

Like the masochist I was turning into, I stood there, watching. My stomach churned more and more the longer I stood there. I knew I should look away, but like a person watching a train wreck happening right before their eyes, I couldn't. I knew that the results were going to end in tragedy—my tragedy—but I couldn't bring myself to turn away from the sight.

As if the rocker felt my eyes on him, Liam lifted his head. I couldn't see if his eyes were open or not, they were so hooded, but somehow I knew that they were. I could feel his gaze on me, moving like a caress as it traveled over my body.

The chick on his lap was kissing his neck while he continued to play with her tits, but his eyes were glued to me. And my body was responding. As if he were touching me. As if we were the ones practically fucking in the middle of a room full of three hundred people.

I wasn't sure what would have happened if Jesse hadn't shifted again and blocked Liam from my line of sight. When his wide shoulders moved to hide the two people sexing up the place, I couldn't help what happened next.

One second I was standing there with a bottle of water in my hand, the next I was bent in half, retching out everything that was in my stomach.

The people standing closest to me moved away, but no one seemed to pay me any attention. I was thankful for that much, at least. When the heaving stopped I rushed to the ladies room to clean up. My heart was racing, my stomach still churning. All I wanted was to go back to the tour bus and take a long, hot shower.

I felt dirty. So fucking dirty. How could I have just stood there, letting him affect me like that? Letting him seduce me even while he had some other woman on his lap, basically dry-humping him?

Dio, I was so fucked up.

I washed my mouth out and threw some cold water on my face before forcing myself to leave the bathroom. I couldn't stay at the club while everyone else partied. Not now. I'd grab a cab back to the buses...

That was the only thought I had in my mind—the only one I allowed myself to have—as I left the bathroom.

The rock god standing outside the ladies room when I stepped out surprised me. Axton was leaning against the opposite wall, arms crossed over his leanly muscled chest. His face was full of concern as he ran hazel eyes over me.

"You okay?" he finally asked after nearly a full minute.

I shrugged. "Drank too much."

His brows lifted, but he didn't call me out on what we both knew was a lie. Pushing off the wall, he moved toward me, only stopping when he was less than a foot away. "Look, you seem like a cool chick. You rock hard, and I'm really into your sound on stage. Fuck, I wouldn't even mind collaborating with you on something."

My eyes widened. To have Axton Cage say something like that was more than a compliment. With his success and status, just having someone important hear him say something like that could make the difference in being at the top of the totem pole or the bottom in the rock world.

He wasn't done, though. "I don't want to see you fuck all of that up, though. I can tell there's something between you and Liam, but trust me when I tell you that he's not where you want to go right now, Brie. He's fucked up, in more ways than you will ever know. Don't mess up your life, your career, over him."

I blinked, slightly touched that he was concerned about me, but more than a little pissed that he thought he needed to protect me.

"Thanks for the advice," I bit out, "but I'm a big girl. I can handle it."

Axton's lips twisted into a grim smile. "If you say so, little girl." Laughing, he shook his head and turned around, going into the men's room. "If you say so," he repeated with another laugh.

Chapter Six

Gabriella

SEVEN YEARS EARLIER

My favorite way to start the day wasn't with a cup of coffee, or a run, or even a really delicious breakfast. It was with a shower. It didn't matter if I'd showered the night before, I couldn't start my day without one. I loved the feeling of being clean, of having the water running over my soapy skin, waking up every part of my body.

The shower on my bus was tiny. No, it was smaller than tiny. My petite body felt crammed into the small box that was that pathetic excuse for a shower and I couldn't imagine how the guys in my band must have felt. Still, I didn't care. I enjoyed every minute of being under the water, even if I was limited to a five-minute shower each morning so that the others could get one in as well.

This morning I stumbled half blind to the bathroom. Normally, I locked the door, because the guys I shared a bus with were still learning boundaries. They'd toured with another singer before, but it had always been a dude, so they hadn't worried about walking in on one another while they were in the bathroom. I couldn't bother myself to spare the energy for that menial action this particular morning, though.

We were just days away from wrapping up the European tour and moving on to Australia. I was exhausted from performing almost every night and then partying until nearly dawn before crawling into bed while the driver drove the bus to whatever stop, in whatever country we were supposed to be in the next night. I'd come to realize that touring is not nearly as much fun as I had always imagined it would be.

Of course, it didn't help that I had to see Liam-Fucking-Bryant with a different chick every damn night. That he didn't care about having public sex right in front of me. Some nights, when I would see him with his new flavor of the night, it felt like he was putting on a show just for me. As if he were trying to hurt me on purpose.

I hated that he had the power to hurt me like that, and I still didn't understand why he had the power to do it in the first place.

Last night had been the worst to-date. I'd seen him getting high in the limo as we'd all gone to yet another nightclub. It wasn't pretty, watching him put that shit up his nose. Witnessing it should have turned me off of him—you would think, at least. All it had done was made me want to help him, made me want to soothe whatever demons haunted him.

Fuck, I was pathetic.

I'd tried to stay away from him all night, but it felt like every time I turned around he was there, sucking face with a different chick. I'd started tossing back one shot after another and looking for someone who would distract me from the hurt that Liam was causing me.

When I'd run straight into Axton Cage coming out of the bathrooms, it had been fate. Over the past nearly three months I'd been getting to know the rock god a little better. Even after he'd warned me off about Liam, he'd remained friendly and yeah, still concerned.

I'd been half drunk when I'd tossed caution to the wind and kissed him. It had been one hell of a kiss. I'd been panting for more when he'd finally pulled back, but no sooner had his lips left mine had my mind gone straight back to what I was so determined to forget.

Axton had brushed one more kiss over my lips before stepping back, a grin on his sexy face. "Now *that* is more like it, little girl. If you want to do it again, come find me."

I hadn't.

Not because I wasn't tempted—because, fuck, who wouldn't have been? Hot rocker wanted me. I hadn't been laid in almost a year. It would have been fun…

I'd gone into the bathroom and done my business. Emmie had been in there, washing her hands. She lifted her chin in a silent greeting before leaving without speaking so much as a word to me. I was still unsure if I liked her or not. There were times she seemed like she would be a fun chick to hang out with. I knew she was loyal to a fault, would cut your throat if you so much as looked like you were going to do something to one of her Demons, and was completely oblivious to the fact that she had at least two guys pining for her. At the very least, two very hot rockers.

Problem was, she didn't seem to get along with anyone but her Demons and Axton Cage. There were two women on the road crew and they both despised Emmie. She was perhaps the biggest bitch I'd ever met, and that included myself.

Still, she hadn't done anything to me, so I was going to remain neutral for the moment.

I was washing my hands when the door to the bathroom opened with a big enough bang to make me jump. Turning to see what the deal was, I felt the air become trapped in my lungs when I saw them.

Some chick in a skirt that let everyone in the club know that she wasn't wearing panties had her legs wrapped around Liam's waist. He was kissing her, squeezing her ass with one hand, and touching her intimately with the other. Bile rose in the back of my throat when he turned around and lifted his head.

At first his gaze went to the five stalls, all of which were empty since the night was wearing down. A lot of the other club goers had already left for the night. Then, as if he realized I was standing there, he turned his blue eyes on me. For what felt like the longest time he just stood there, staring at me while the chick in his arms continued to kiss every part of him he would let her kiss.

Liam blinked and smirked at me. "Wanna join us?"

The girl in his arms giggled but I wanted to throw up. I wasn't going to let him know that, though. He seemed to get off on making me hurt, and if he knew he was killing me right then, he would love it. Forcing a grin to my lips, I pulled a few paper towels from the dispenser and dried my hands. "Nah, big guy. You have fun, though." I tossed the wet paper towels in the trash as I moved toward the door. "*Ciao*, Liam."

After that, I hadn't been able to stay a second longer. I'd gone outside and taken a cab back to my empty bus before crawling into bed and stupidly crying myself to sleep. Now, as I stood under the spray of the shower, mentally washing away those pictures from my mind as I washed my body, I tried not to cry again.

Fuck, I was not *that* girl. I wasn't the kind of chick to let a douchebag beat me up emotionally like this. He obviously didn't want me. It had been thrown in my face for nearly three full months now. It was time I got over it, over him, and the fact that he didn't want anything to do with me.

From now on, I wasn't going to let Liam Bryant fuck with my heart anymore…

Ah, shit. My fingers stilled in my hair, suds half blinding me, but that didn't matter. Not when the real reason for why Liam had so much power to hurt me finally hit me so hard. I was in love with him.

"No!" I cried and pounded my fist on the shower wall. "No way."

I decided then and there that even if I did love that bastard rocker, I wasn't going to let it bother me anymore. It was time I moved on, found a lover, and fucked Liam out of my head and my heart.

Rinsing my hair, I scrubbed the rest of my body until my skin was pink and tingling. I was just about to cut off the water when the bathroom door opened so suddenly that I didn't have time to shield my body.

Startled, I wiped water from my eyes to find Martin standing in the small bathroom watching me with eyes that were bright with a desire that turned my stomach nearly as much as seeing Liam with other girls had. Belatedly, I covered my breasts with my one arm and opened the shower door to grab my towel before finally turning off the water.

"Get out!" I yelled at him.

Martin licked his lips, his hands going straight to the top of his sweatpants and pushing them down his narrow hips. I might want a lover, but it was definitely not going to be this creep. "Get. The. Fuck. Out!" I screamed.

"Come on, Gabriella. You know you don't mean that." Martin had his pants down now and he wasn't wearing any underwear. When I saw his erection, I nearly gaged and started screaming again. "I've seen those sexy little looks you send me. You want this, babe."

"Get out, you stupid sonofabitch. You repulse me. Get out!"

He threw his head back and laughed. One hand wrapped around his dick and he started stroking himself. Fucking gross. I hated this guy. No way I wanted him. He was crazy if he thought I would ever give him any reason to think I would ever—*ever*—want his nasty ass.

"Stop playing hard to get, Gabriella. You got me, babe. I'm all yours." He took a step toward me and I realized several things all at once. One, he really was mental. Two, no way were the other guys on the bus. I'd just screamed this place down, yelling at Martin and calling him names that should have had the other three rushing to see what was going on. With the exception of the creep now standing in front of me, the other three guys in my band were decent men. They had all told me to let them know if I ever needed anything, but especially let them know if anyone gave me any problems. And three…

This guy was going to rape me if I didn't do something to protect myself.

That thought had everything inside of me going stone cold. I tightened my hold on my towel and refused to cower like some scared little girl facing down the big, bad wolf. No way was this guy going to hurt me. I refused to become a victim.

Thinking fast, I tried to relax. Best form of action was to act like I wanted what Martin thought he could give me. When he got close enough, I was going to knee him in the balls. I pictured him falling to his knees and then completely to the floor where I would kick the shit out of him.

Another step forward and Martin was almost close enough for me to raise my knee and make him wish he'd never been born a man. Bile was choking me, rising more and more with each breath I inhaled and smelled Martin's cologne. He'd always worn too much, and I'd always thought it smelled like old-man aftershave mixed with ass.

He stopped. Letting go of his dick, he lifted the hand he'd been holding himself with to touch my face. I smelled the muskiness on his skin and all plans of kicking the shit out of him went flying out of my head with the contents of my stomach as I bent over and puked my guts out.

Martin jumped back but not in time to avoid getting sprayed with the revolting bile as I practically projectile vomited all down his stomach, dick, and legs.

When the bathroom door suddenly opened—more like it was jerked off its hinges—I couldn't help the startled scream that left my lips. Martin groaned seconds before I heard flesh hitting flesh and then Martin slumped to the floor, nearly falling into my mess. Still bent in half, trying to catch my breath after emptying the contents of my stomach onto the floor, I tried to lift my head enough to see what was going on.

The first thing I saw was a pair of boots, and they were kicking the shit out of the now unconscious Martin. Straightening, I focused on the man who had just saved me and nearly vomited again.

Liam.

With one more kick to Martin's midsection, Liam stepped back. He turned his wild, blue eyes on me. They raked over my towel-clad body, taking in the puke on the floor before going back to where my breasts were nearly popping out of the top of the towel. He was breathing hard, his face dark with rage, and his eyes glazed with a brightness that told me that he was high.

"You okay?" he finally asked after what felt like a lifetime of standing there staring at me.

I shrugged. Was I? I didn't know. My brain was having trouble processing everything all of a sudden. One minute I'd been about to be attacked, the next I was puking my guts out and Liam Bryant was saving me.

Liam shook out his hand and I noticed that his knuckles were bleeding. "That fucker's got a glass jaw, that's for sure. Dropped like the pussy he is with just one hit." He stepped over Martin's motionless body and held out his other hand to me. "Come on, little Brie. Let's get you away from this ugliness."

I blinked down at his hand. What? How? Why?

So many questions were running through my mind and I didn't have the answers to them. Fingers trembling, I finally took his hand and he held it firm but so damn tenderly as he helped me step over my bassist—my ex-bassist. No way was I going to let him stay on this tour with us any longer. No fucking way.

Out of the bathroom now, Liam guided me down the narrow hall to the roosts. He opened the closet that we all shared and reached inside without releasing my hand. Mutely, I stood there, shivering in my damp towel. After only a few moments he pulled out a bra, panties, top, and jeans. He placed them on the first bunk he came to and only then did he release me.

The hand that had been holding mine so gently lifted and he pushed my dripping hair back from my face. "Get dressed, sweetheart."

I stood there, stunned for long minutes after he'd closed the door behind him. I could hear him just on the other side, as if he were waiting on me, ready to protect me again if he needed to. He must have been on his phone, because all I could hear was him speaking, and he sounded pissed.

Honestly, I didn't know what to think after what had just happened. Liam Bryant had just saved me. How had he known? Why had he saved me? Why was he still here?

From what little I'd learned about him over the last three months, I knew that he wasn't the type of guy who usually stuck his neck out for anyone. He was normally trapped in his own little world, high off his ass. Life seemed to pass him by and I hadn't seen even one little clue as to him actually giving a flying fuck about it.

Which only confused me that much more. Why was I attracted to someone like him? Why was I so sure that I was in love with him? It blew my mind that I was so hung up over a guy that was so damaged. I wasn't the type of chick who wanted to be the one to fix some broken guy. Normally, I was completely turned off by a guy who didn't have his life figured out.

Yet, here I was, still standing in the middle of the sleep quarters on my tiny tour bus in nothing more than a damp towel and falling that much more in love with a guy who was so fucked up there wasn't even a word invented that properly described his fucked-up-ness.

Liam's voice got louder, angrier, and I quickly started dressing. My hair was a soaking wet mess, but I didn't care. I dried it with the wet towel as well as I could and finally opened the door that separated me from Liam.

He stood there with his phone pressed to his ear, yelling at whoever was on the other end. When those blue eyes lifted to me, he abruptly broke off and the hand holding the cellphone dropped to his side. "Okay?" I nodded, unable to find my voice just yet. "Good. Emmie is going to get this piece of shit out of here and find you someone to replace him for the remainder of the tour. Don't worry about anything, okay? She's better than any one of those fucking gods she swears by. Chick can move mountains with just her little finger when she sets her mind to it."

The admiration I heard in his voice had something tightening and twisting in my chest. It was the first time I'd ever heard anything other than bored disinterest or amusement in his voice. Was Liam in love with Emmie Jameson just like half the other guys on this fucking tour were?

Clenching my jaw, I pushed down the sudden shot of jealousy that threatened to choke me and forced a small smile to my lips. "Okay," I murmured. "Thanks, Liam. For... Well, just thanks."

His eyes darkened even more. "I heard you screaming for him to get out. Sorry I didn't get to you sooner, but the door was locked and I had to break the damn thing to get in."

"I—" I broke off when my voice cracked. It was hard to imagine what might have happened if Liam hadn't heard me. "Thank you for checking on me."

His lips lifted at the corners in a grim smile. "Don't thank me, Brie. I would never walk away from a chick in danger. Just thinking about it makes me mental. If something like that happened to my sister and no one helped her…" He shook his head. "I would go insane. No way am I going to let it happen to anyone else."

From the front of the bus I could hear people coming aboard. I heard Emmie's voice followed by Doug and then Jesse Thornton, both Stevenson brothers, Nik Armstrong, and Axton Cage. All of them were talking at once as they filled up my small living room and I knew I had to go out there and talk to them.

I just wished I could stop everything and stay there just talking to Liam for a few more minutes. The look on his face as he'd mentioned his sister, the way his voice had changed when he'd spoken of her, told me that no matter what kind of man he was, his sister was the most important person in his life.

Maybe he wasn't as broken as I'd first thought…

Chapter Rock Seven

Liam

She was out of surgery and back in ICU once again.

The doctor and two nurses had come out to speak to us two hours ago. They had found the fragment of the .22-caliber bullet they had missed the first time. It had been hiding behind her heart. Dr. Schiller hadn't tried to sugarcoat anything that he told us and I was still unsure if I was glad that he had given it to me straight or not.

I'd nearly vomited when he'd told me what had happened when he'd opened up Gabriella's chest—for the second time. He'd lost her. Twice.

Two times my little Italian goddess had tried to leave this world again. Two fucking times. Schiller had been able to bring her back and the rest of the surgery had been a success with no further complications. He still wasn't changing her odds, however. It could still go either way.

Gabriella was in critical condition. Only time and God could tell if she would make it through this.

After the doctor and his nurses had left, with the promise of letting me back to see her once she was settled in ICU, I'd fallen back into the chair I'd been sitting in since Alexis had arrived. My friends and family tried to speak to me but I couldn't hear any of them. Not one word penetrated my mind.

All I could see was her face as I'd screamed at her to get out of my own hospital room when I'd woken up from my car wreck. Would she kick me out when she woke up from this? Would she not want to see me, speak to me, *love me* when she opened those beautiful brown eyes and saw me?

I decided it didn't matter. If she yelled at me like I'd yelled at her, I wouldn't leave. It would take all of Seller's gorillas in suits to pull me out of this hospital.

Someone pushed a cup of coffee into my hands and I finally lifted my eyes from where I'd been staring sightlessly for the past two hours or more. When I realized it was Annabelle and that she was now sitting beside me drinking her own coffee, I frowned. "Thanks," I muttered before taking a swallow of the hot drink. It was weak and tasted more like ass than coffee, but it warmed a small part of my insides, unthawed my body enough that I felt like I wasn't going to freeze to death.

"You doing okay?" she asked, taking another sip of her own coffee.

"Ask me again in a few days. If Gabriella makes it through this, then I'll be fine. If…" I shrugged, unable to finish. Unable to speak aloud my worst fears.

Annabelle nodded, understanding without me having to say the words. "You've changed, Liam. It's nice to see what a good man you turned into after seeing what a fucked-up boy you were. Tawny really destroyed you."

I gritted my teeth as thoughts of the chick who had been so many of my firsts flitted through my mind. First love. First kiss. First chick I'd ever fucked. She'd been my high school sweetheart, the girl who had initiated me into manhood.

The chick to give me my first taste of coke.

Tawny's uncle had been a small-time drug dealer in Nashville. I hadn't known until I was already hooked on the shit that she helped him deal coke, meth, weed, even pills. If I had been smart, I would have walked away from her then, but I'd been in love.

In love with the drugs.

It had taken me years to realize that it was the drugs I'd been in love with and not Tawny. When I'd realized it, I'd been about to break up with her when she'd told me she was pregnant. So we'd stayed together and, for the first time in my life, I'd found something other than the drugs or my sister that had touched my heart.

I thought I was going to be a father.

I saw the ultrasounds, went to almost every prenatal appointment. No one would ever claim that I wasn't committed to being a dad. I'd loved that baby so damn much. I still did.

When Harris was laid in my arms, he'd been the most beautiful little baby I'd ever seen. When the nurse had told me his blood type, and I'd taken a closer look—saw my best friend's face in that face that I loved so much—I'd gone a little insane.

It was because of the drugs that I'd been able to deal with Devlin being Harris's father. They blocked out the pain as my heart had been torn from my chest every time I'd seen the little boy I'd thought was going to be my own. Over the years, as I'd watched that little boy grow—watched the small nightmare that his mother had made of his life as she'd played tug of war with Devlin, using Harris as the rope—my heart had broken a little more. And I'd escaped more and more into the drugs.

When I'd finally gotten clean, was ready to stay clean, I'd had to deal with all of that pain. That was when I'd realized that Devlin hadn't been to blame for all that shit back then. Tawny had drugged him and tricked him into sleeping with her to get pregnant because I never had sex with her without protection. Never. The only way she'd been able to claim Harris was mine in the first place was because she'd swore up and down that one of the condoms had broken.

Not wanting to go down memory lane with Annabelle about my fucked-up past, I turned toward her. "How has life been treating you, Anna-Banana?"

Her lips twitched as if she were fighting a smile at my old nickname for her. "No one's called me that in over seventeen years." She took another swallow of her coffee, grimacing at the taste, and blew out a tired sigh. "Life hasn't been too hard on me. I've helped Noah with his career, took over as his manager for the last six years. When he decided to retire from all of this last year, I decided to take on a few other musicians. Six months ago I ran into Gabriella. Her contract with Craig was up and she decided to give me a shot."

My eyes narrowed on the woman, remembering the girl she'd once been. "Why do I get the feeling that you're leaving a lot out, Anna-Banana?"

Her eyes drifted across the room and I followed her gaze to the group standing by one of the windows. Natalie, Devlin, Zander, and Kenzie were standing there talking in quiet tones. I knew which of them she was looking at, though, and reached for her hand, giving it a firm squeeze, bringing her eyes back to me.

Annabelle shook her head as if to clear it. "That was a long time ago."

"Maybe." I didn't say what I really wanted to say, though. That it might have been a long time ago, but sometimes time doesn't mean shit when your heart was involved.

Her phone buzzed and she took one look at the screen before jumping up like the room was on fire and rushing out the door without another word to me. Alone again, I scrubbed my hands over my face, realizing that they were still trembling, and balled them into fists.

Where was that fucking nurse? When could I see Gabriella again? Fucking hell, all I wanted was to tell her I loved her one more goddamn time. See her eyes. Have her heat chase away the cold that was numbing every part of my body. I was going out of my mind and nothing and no one could fix it but her.

My eyes closed and I tried to think positive thoughts. She was going to be okay. She had to be okay. Fuck what her grandfather said. I didn't give a shit anymore. Gabriella was what I wanted, what I needed. And if she still wanted me, still loved me even a little, I would take that. I'd hold on and never let that girl go again.

Cold, soft fingers touched my arm. Slowly I opened my eyes to find Alexis standing over me with Jordan in her arms. When had her son arrived? Behind her stood her husband and her brother, Vince Sheppard. He was a doctor, the best spinal surgeon in the country. Even though Gabriella wasn't his cousin, since he and Alexis were only half siblings, I knew that he cared about her.

"The nurse just said we could go back. They are going to let me take Vince with me since he's a doctor, but I don't want to go back without you." She kissed her son's cheek before handing him over to his father, and then reached for my hand. Together our hands made a block of ice, but her touch comforted me more than any of my friends and family could. This was the only person Gabriella would kill for. Having her there with me made it the tiniest bit better.

Standing, I walked with her toward the door but couldn't help but look back to find Dallas. Would they let me take her back there too? She would know what was going on in there. Be able to read the machines and tell me just how bad things still were. Her tired blue eyes were watching me and as if she could read the silent plea in my own eyes, she stood and followed after us.

Inside the ICU, a nurse was standing by the door, waiting on us. Vince spoke quietly to her and she nodded, leading the four of us back to the room Gabriella had been in hours before. Everything looked the same to me. She was still lying in that damn bed, looking so small and pale. Machines were making all kinds of racket, but I would never find them annoying ever again. Those noises meant that she was alive, that she was still fighting to stay with me.

Alexis still held onto my hand, but she was starting to shake as she gazed down at her cousin. Her brother wrapped his arm around her waist to help steady her and we eased her into the only chair beside the bed. Tears were running down her face as she whispered something brokenly in Italian that I didn't understand.

Dallas moved around to the other side of the bed where all the machines were hooked up. She frowned as she looked from one machine to another. I was scared to ask her what she thought, what her professional opinion was.

"Well?" Alexis whispered

Dallas shrugged before letting her shoulders droop tiredly again. "Her heart rate is low and her O2 isn't much better. Her chest tube looks good. I'm just wondering how much blood they've given her already."

Vince nodded. "Yeah. Let's go talk to the nurses."

As Dallas passed me, she gave my shoulder a squeeze before following him out to the nurses' station. I swallowed hard and crouched down next to Alexis, not giving a damn that sitting like that was agony on my leg.

"Even like this, she's the most beautiful woman I've ever seen," I murmured.

"Yes," Alexis breathed out on a broken sob.

Neither of us spoke after that. Just sat there, both of us silently crying unashamedly as we watched Gabriella's chest rise and fall slowly. Time passed, I wasn't even sure how much. Vince returned, without Dallas, and whispered something in his sister's ear that had her shaking her head adamantly. He muttered a curse and left again, but we didn't move.

Vince didn't come back, but a nurse came in carrying another chair, shocking me enough that I straightened. My leg was one big throb, but I didn't give a shit.

She set the chair in front of me with a grim smile. "As long as the two of you don't get in our way or cause trouble, you can stay. Dr. Sheppard arranged it with Dr. Schiller." I eased myself down into the chair she had brought and grasped Alexis's hand once more. "It's okay, you know. You can talk to her. Let her know that the two of you are here. It might help."

I nodded and the nurse left. Once again the room was silent except for the noises coming from the machines Gabriella was hooked to. We could have sat there for minutes, hours, even days. I wouldn't have noticed the passing of time. My eyes were glued to my girl, silently willing her to live.

A different nurse came in, changed out the bag of blood and the fluids that were attached to the IV. She didn't speak to us as she did her job and then left.

My eyes were starting to feel heavy and I finally glanced over at Alexis to check on her. As if my movement pulled her out of a funny memory, she let out a soft laugh. "You know, I was always curious as to why Gabs hates Emmie. She never would tell me, and I always assumed it was over Axton, but after he married Dallas, I wasn't so sure."

I blew out a breath that was full of self-loathing. "It wasn't because of Axton," I admitted. "It wasn't even Emmie's fault, actually. That was all on me. I asked Em to do it."

Alexis's eyes widened. "Really? But you two weren't even together back then."

"Yeah, but that was because I figured I wasn't good enough for her. Then later on, I decided I didn't care if I was good enough or not. I wanted her, loved her."

She reached out and took hold of her cousin's hand for the first time. When the heart monitor made a loud protest, we both jumped, but Alexis didn't release Gabriella's hand. Her hold tightened and she turned her attention back to me. "So tell me why Gabs hates her."

"I let her think that I was into Emmie…" I began, hating myself all over again for putting those thoughts in Gabriella's head. Back then I'd been so lost in the drugs and fighting my feelings hard for a little Italian goddess. I fought them tooth and nail, ran from them, and even then I was starting to cave.

By using Emmie, I'd finally been able to push her far enough away. And right into Axton's arms…

Gabriella

One second it felt like I was floating, wondering if I was in purgatory or some other crazy shit. The next I had the most amazing feeling of peace wash over me. I tried to smile but my lips refused to cooperate.

"Tell me why Gabs hates her," I thought I heard my Lee-Lee saying.

If my eyes had been working, they would have filled with tears at the sound of my beloved cousin's bell-like voice. I was a fucked-up piece of shit, but with Alexis I felt like I was a better person. She grounded me. Made me see the world through different eyes. That chick was the best part of me. The only goodness I had in my heart was because of her.

Her and Jordan.

My heart clenched at the thought of my little 'nephew'. I loved him like he was my own. I would have given just about anything to have been able to open my eyes and see that little man right then.

"I let her think I was into Emmie."

At the sound of *his* voice, all thoughts of Alexis and Jordan evaporated. I strained to hear every word he spoke. If only I could see him, touch him.

Make him love me again.

With each word that came from that voice I loved so much, I felt like I could picture the day that I'd realized that Emmie Jameson was never going to be my friend. Not when the guy I was stupidly in love with was in love with her.

SEVEN YEARS EARLIER

I didn't know how the bitch did it, but Emmie found me a new bass player before our next show. Hank was a forty-one-year-old who had been playing bass since he was ten years old. He blew me away with his skills and I knew by the second show that I wasn't ever getting rid of that man.

Ever since the incident in the bathroom, I'd been trying to put what Martin could have done to me out of my head, but nearly being attacked was not something that I could just erase from my head. I'd asked to have extra locks put on the bathroom door of the tour bus we were given in Australia.

Even better was that this new bus had one private bedroom as well as the usual roosts. Before I could even demand it, Doug and the others were putting my stuff in there. It also had extra locks on the door and I was able to sleep somewhat peacefully knowing I was safe behind a locked door.

If only my heart was so easily protected.

The scolding I'd given myself about loving Liam Bryant might as well have never happened. My heart hadn't listened. Or maybe it had and when he'd saved me it had just refused to accept what my brain kept trying to tell it.

Stupid heart.

So he'd saved me. So what? It didn't matter. He'd only done it because he didn't want a female getting hurt if he could stop it. It sure as hell hadn't been because he cared about me.

That much was made evident three weeks into the Australian tour. After our first concert we were once again out on the town. Twenty minutes at the bar where we had the whole place all to ourselves—along with two hundred fans—I'd gone looking for Liam.

I'd seen him talking to Nik and Drake earlier so I started there first. Axton was sitting with the two Demons and winked when I approached the three rockers. "If I knew you were gonna wear something like that tonight, I would have invited you to my bus and we could have avoided all this shit."

A grin teased at my lips. He might not be the one my heart said I wanted, but I was starting to warm up to the rock god. He flirted a lot, drank often, and tried to hide his real feelings for a chick I realized was more his best friend than anything else. Axton was also a nice guy. That was hard to find in my world, so I'd stopped spitting on the small friendship we were making.

"Damn," I muttered with a wink. "There's always next time."

I sat down on the edge of his chair. He knew what I was there for, and even though his eyes darkened with concern he still leaned into me. "Saw him go toward the bathrooms," he muttered low enough that his Demon friends couldn't hear.

"Alone?" No way in hell was I going to chase after him tonight if he was hooking up with someone.

Axton shrugged. "He wasn't with anyone when he went that way. Doesn't mean he doesn't have someone back there now."

My gut twisted and some of my courage in seeking him out faded. Did I really want to chance going back there and finding him with someone else? Was he really worth that?

Muttering a curse, because the only answer to that was a resounding 'yes', I kissed Axton's cheek and stood. "Later," I called over my shoulder to the three rockers and headed straight for the bathrooms.

The bathrooms were in the back of the club, and of course down a narrow, dimly lit hall. Each was in their own little alcove at the end. The closer I got to them the more my heart raced. My hands began to sweat and I was sure that I was going to be sick. What would I do if I found him with another chick?

Jealousy ate at me like a cancer as I clenched my jaw and forced myself to walk faster. As I rounded the corner, I nearly ran into Liam's back. Stopping less than a few inches away from him, I breathed out a relieved sigh.

He was standing in front of the ladies room, and for a moment I thought he was alone.

Until he lowered his head and kissed some chick with red hair. Stunned, I stood there, almost entranced as I watched him kiss her like he'd never kissed anyone that I could remember witnessing. It wasn't his normal 'I want to eat your face' kind of kiss. It was sweet, tender…loving.

Less than ten seconds later he lifted his head, blocking out the sight of the chick he was with. One hand lifted and I just knew that he was stroking her face. "I love you."

Sucking in a pain-filled breath, I turned and ran, not stopping until I reached the bar. Ordering a double shot of tequila, I swallowed the entire thing in one go, before turning to glare at the hall I'd just came from.

Who the fuck was Liam in love with? He didn't do love. Just hookups.

Dropping the glass on the bar top, I demanded another just as a redhead left the hall that led to the bathrooms. She was dressed in a Demon's Wings shirt with a hole in the shoulder, and jeans that were so faded there was barely any thread left at the knees. Her hair was in disarray, as if someone had been running his fingers through it.

No. No way.

Not her. Not. Fucking. Her.

Sure, I'd seen the way Liam looked at her. As if he was in awe of her, but I'd thought he just admired her. I'd never really suspected that he could have been in love with her.

Yet, there she was, walking across the bar toward Jesse Thornton, combing her fingers through her wild hair. She was small enough to have been the chick Liam had been with just a few minutes ago. And it wouldn't be like he was the only man in love with that little bitch. Every guy on tour with us—band member or roadie—wanted a piece of that ass. I knew two rockers who were in love with her for sure.

Still, I'd been sure that she was oblivious to all of that. She might be a hard-ass, but something about her had screamed at me that she was an innocent. The chick was a virgin, for sure. I would have bet good money on it.

Now I wasn't sure.

Maybe she was one of those types that got off on making guys want her, fall for her, and tease them with what they couldn't have before finally giving in. It wouldn't surprise me, but I'd thought I'd pegged her differently.

Especially since I'd seen more than once the way she looked at Nik Armstrong when he wasn't looking. She was in love with that particular rocker, and I was pretty sure he was in love with her.

So why was she playing games with Liam?

In that moment, I hated her. I hated Liam too, for being so stupid to fall in love with a chick who couldn't love him the way he deserved. But I hated Emmie even more.

I was still steaming over it the next day as I came back from rehearsing with my band before that night's show. As I headed back toward my bus, I caught sight of Emmie and her fucking clipboard as she moved from one table to the next, checking off something on one of her endless lists.

Stopping, I stood there, watching her. I wondered how she would feel if someone hurt her the way I was sure she was going to hurt Liam. She didn't love him, not when she was so in love with Nik. That bitch was just going to lead him on and break his heart.

The thought of him hurting like that made my chest ache even as jealousy churned in my gut. No. I couldn't let her go on like that and not show her how much that kind of pain would hurt.

Before I realized what I was going to do, I was walking toward her.

"You should have told me that Nik was so talented with his mouth. If I'd known sooner, I wouldn't have waited so long to take a ride on the rocker." The words popped out before I even knew I was going to say them.

Emmie's head snapped up at the first sound of my voice and I watched as her face went from somewhat welcoming to ice cold and full of hate. I didn't miss the flash of pain that filled those big green eyes before she lowered her lashes. "Excuse me?" Her voice was deceptively soft, but I knew that she'd heard me. The trembling in her hands told me that she wasn't as unaffected as she wanted everyone around us to believe.

I grinned at her. There was a few inches difference in our heights, but while she was taller, I was much curvier. I wouldn't willingly admit it out loud, but I outweighed the bitch by at least fifteen pounds. "Yeah, he definitely knows how to use that mouth for more than just singing. Man's got one talented tongue. I'm seriously thinking about going back for seconds. What do you think? Should I jump back on for another ride? He wants me to, but I just don't know if I should."

The ever-present clipboard fell to the cement floor with a loud bang and I knew my grin was turning more evil by the second. I'd hit my mark, made my point. Emmie was hurting and I could see the same hate I felt for her filling those beautiful eyes.

Along with the hate, I also saw the rage, and her slender hands balled into fists seconds before a big, bald Demon caught her around the waist and carried her away. Jesse was muttering something to Emmie that I couldn't hear, but I didn't care what it was. I'd hurt her as much as I knew she was going to hurt Liam.

As much as *I* was hurting, because I knew that as long as Liam loved her, he would never want me.

Liam

I sat with Alexis beside Gabriella's bed for two hours before she had to go back out to the waiting room. Jordan was getting upset, wanting both his mother and his Aunt Gabs. His father and uncle couldn't console him so she went out to hold him for a little while.

As much as I had been glad to have Alexis sitting with me, helping me through this as much as I was helping her, I was thankful to be alone with Gabriella. The moment she was gone, I pulled my chair closer to the side of the bed and lifted my girl's cold hand to my lips.

"I don't know if you can hear me or not, little Brie, but I'm really hoping you can." My lips lingered over her ring finger and I closed my eyes. If I hadn't been such a fucking stupid screw-up, my ring would have already been on this chick's finger. All I'd had to do was stop being a pussy when I first met her and we could have been married with who knew how many kids running around. "If you don't hear me, though, as soon as you open those damn beautiful eyes I'll repeat everything I'm about to tell you now."

Blowing out a tired breath, I stroked my thumb over the back of her hand. "I'm sorry I wasted so much time, Brie. I'm sorry that you thought I didn't want you, or that I didn't love you. I think I fell for you the second we knocked into each other, but you scared the ever-loving fuck out of me. I knew the first time I saw you kissing Axton that I'd made a mistake by pushing you away, but by then it was too late. I had to live with the fact that I'd pushed you at my friend and waited impatiently for you two to end."

I'd waited three months before Gabriella had dumped Axton the first time. But by the time I'd been clear-minded enough to realize they were no longer a thing, they had gotten back together. Another two months passed before they had another argument and broke up again. That was the pattern for over two years. It had driven me crazy and I'd hidden more and more in my only solace.

Drugs.

It wasn't until Axton had taken the judging gig for *America's Rocker* and gotten with Dallas that I realized it was finally over with them for good. I'd invited myself to New York and crashed with my bandmate with the sole intention of hooking up with Gabriella Moreitti. That night had really not gone as I'd planned, but I'd gotten my first taste of my little Italian goddess and, after that, I'd found something that was just as addicting as the drugs I poisoned my body with.

I brushed another kiss over the back of Gabriella's hand, watching while her chest slowly rose with each breath the machine was helping her take. Lifting my gaze to her face, I felt my eyes sting at how pale she was. There were blue shadows under her eyes, making me wonder if she was in any pain. Her lips were dry around the tube in her mouth that was helping her breathe and I reminded myself to make sure the nurse put something on them the next time she came in.

With my free hand, I skimmed my fingers over her cheek as a few tears spilled from my eyes. I don't think I'd ever really cried in my life until now, until this. Fear of losing the most important person in someone's life was enough to make anyone cry like a damn baby, though. Clearing my throat because I didn't want her to hear my tears and be upset if she really could hear me, I whispered her name. "Brie…" My voice cracked and I used my shoulder to wipe away the tears that were now streaming down my face. They wouldn't stop and I really didn't give a fuck. "…remember the night I finally made you mine? I was a stupid fucker back then, huh? It took me too long to make a move and when I did, I messed it up by letting you leave without me. If... When. *When* you open your eyes, I'll make all of that up to you. I swear I'll spend the rest of my life making it up to you."

Gabriella

"Remember that night, Brie?"

I wanted to tell him I remembered, wanted to tell him so damn much about the night that had gone so wrong on so many levels. The best part of one of the worst nights of my life was being with him, but then things had gotten crazy. Lines had been blurred and crossed and I'd nearly ruined more than one life that night.

His thumb felt rough against my cheek but so soft I knew if I could cry, I'd have been sobbing like a baby right then. His touch was so soothing to my aching soul and all I wanted was to open my eyes and tell him that none of it mattered. The past could go fuck itself, for all I cared. I just wanted a future with the man I loved.

When he spoke again, it was about that night and once again I felt the pull of those memories pull me away from the present. Away from the pain in my chest that was a mixture of physical and emotional that made it difficult to draw in a deep enough breath.

FOUR YEARS EARLIER

I was two glasses of Italian wine into dinner when I got the text. When I saw who it was from, I nearly choked on the mouthful I'd been about to swallow.

This was a joke. Right?

Liam never texted me. Never called. Never...anything. In the last two years I'd done my best to push him out of my head and my stupid heart. Axton had helped, for the most part. The sex had been amazing, but that was really all there had been to our relationship.

Lots of sex, plenty of arguing as we'd both tried to pretend we had deeper feelings for each other that were more than just friendship. We both knew that it wasn't going to last from day one. Even when he'd gotten that damn tattoo, my name on his wrist, I hadn't believed he was actually in love with me.

The ink had pretty much been a nail in the coffin for me. It wasn't even my name. Just *Brie*. He was one of the handful of people who called me by that damn nickname Liam had given me, and he'd put it on his flesh for the world to see. All it did was remind me of Liam. I knew that it was Axton's way of trying to convince the world that he wasn't in love with his best friend, and if it had been anyone but Emmie Jameson I wouldn't have cared.

But the facts wouldn't change. He was in love with Emmie and I just couldn't deal with that. Not when she had good guys like Axton panting after her and bad boys like Liam pining for her from afar. She made me sick. All I wanted was to punch her in the tit a few good times because she did nothing but twist guys into knots over her.

N town. Party @ Axton's. Hope u come.

I read the text again and gulped down the rest of the wine in my glass. He wanted me to come to a party at Axton's house? It wouldn't have been the first time I'd gone to Axton's apartment to just hang out since our last—and final—breakup. None of those times had Liam been there. He was usually in Tennessee with his sister. From what I'd heard over the years, Liam hated New York. So why was he in town?

Even as I was wondering, my heart was pounding, my palms growing damp with a mixture of anxiety and excitement. Shaking my head, I poured myself another glass of the rich Italian wine Alexis's husband had sent me as a peace offering the day Jordan had been born. We'd decided to put our differences behind us for the sake of his son. I was still struggling not to shoot him in the balls, but for that baby boy I'd refrain from murdering his father. I'd opened it tonight because I'd been bored and honestly needed something good to drink to create the buzz I was looking for. Now, I needed the alcohol for courage.

Should I go? Was it worth torturing myself with seeing Liam? It had taken so damn long to get to a place where I could even think about the man without my chest hurting. What if he had other chicks there and they were all over him? Could I see him, watch him with someone else, and still keep the walls around my heart from cracking and breaking my heart all over again?

I didn't know why I just sat there debating the whole thing with myself. From the second I'd seen that text, I knew I was going to go. Yeah, it was more than apparent that I was a masochist, but I was only hurting myself so who the fuck cared?

I showered, dressed in one of the new dresses my aunt had sent from Milan a few days ago, and put on enough makeup so that I looked hot but didn't scream desperate. I hadn't had sex in months and all I could think about was getting Liam alone. Damn it, I sounded pathetic. I had no pride when it came to that particular rocker.

I took a cab to Axton's place and found people practically spilling out of the apartment when I walked in. It was only six thirty but the place was overflowing with partiers. I pushed my way through, looking for someone I knew. Axton wasn't anywhere in sight but when I finally found Liam, I instantly regretted leaving the safe confines of my living room.

He was sitting on the couch with a shiny silver tray in his lap, two coke-whores on either side of him. He had enough coke on the tray to keep the entire place high for a week, but between him and the four chicks surrounding him, I doubted it would last more than another hour.

With a straw in one of his hands and a slut kissing his neck, I nearly turned around and left. I didn't need this shit tonight. I'd lost what little buzz I'd gotten from the Italian wine the second I'd seen Liam and my heart was already aching from the sight of him destroying himself like that.

Then I spotted a half empty bottle of tequila and figured, what the hell? I was there and even though the sight of the guy I was stupidly in love with basically gutted me, I would make sure I had a good time. I just needed to get drunk and find someone to help take my mind off the fucking asshole.

Somewhere in the mess that was Axton's apartment, I found a clean glass and poured the tequila into it. I gulped down the contents in one swallow before filling it to the rim. I was four glasses in before the first one hit me and the pain in my chest wasn't nearly as hard to accept.

For the next forty-five minutes I drank my way through the rest of the bottle of tequila and then moved onto a fresh one. I hadn't seen Liam again so I moved around the apartment, my emotions a mixture of hurt, lust, need, and anger. I wanted to have hard, angry sex with a complete stranger in my ex's home. It wasn't the answer to my problems, and even through my drunkenness I knew I would regret it in the morning, but right then I didn't give a shit.

I paused in the middle of the living room, looking around for a possible hookup for a meaningless one-night stand. It wasn't my style; normally, I didn't slut myself out like that, but this was different. I was different tonight. I just wanted to fucking forget.

No one caught my attention so I turned around. Maybe there was someone in the kitchen who would interest me…

I bumped into the guy standing just behind me, spilling half my drink and nearly falling on my ass. Strong hands grasped my waist, steadying me, but I still fell against his chest. Looking up I saw that it was someone I knew. "A Demon," I muttered to myself and grinned. "Oh, good. It's the fun one." Then I blinked and sighed. "No, wait. It's the drunk one." Damn it, the Stevenson brothers looked so much alike they could have easily passed as twins. This one was leaner than the other and his hair was longer, so I knew it was Drake. The drunk. Or was that ex-drunk? I wasn't sure. "I was hoping it was the fun one. I really need to get laid."

"I don't think my brother would take you up on your offer," Drake informed me with a glare as he released me. "He knows Emmie would cut off his balls."

I grimaced. "Ah, yes. The sainted Emmie." I rolled my eyes and took another sip of my drink. "Don't want to upset her, now do we?" I snorted out a laugh and walked away, nearly tripping over someone's feet as I headed for the kitchen.

The night passed slowly, or so it felt like to me. I found myself talking to various people. When some leggy blonde showed up with a piece of meat that looked like he belonged on the cover of some muscle magazine, looking like every woman's fantasy come to life, I was sure I'd found my one-nighter.

I swallowed the rest of my drink and moved toward the delicious piece of eye-candy. Before I could reach him, Axton called out to the blonde and wrapped his arms around her waist before kissing her. Maybe I was drunker than I thought because the way he kissed this chick was different. He held onto her as if he didn't ever want to let her go and when he lifted his head there was a look in his eyes that was definitely different.

Huh, good for him. If he was getting over Emmie then I was all for him hooking up with this chick.

I nearly tripped again before I reached the three. Axton's hazel eyes narrowed on me. "Brie?"

I gave him my brightest smile. "Hey, you." I turned my gaze to the big guy standing protectively beside the beautiful blonde. "Hi."

The guy's lips twitched for a second, but never really lifted into an actual smile. "Hi."

"I'm Gabriella."

Axton cleared his throat and grasped my arm. "What are you doing here?"

I shrugged. "Liam invited me." I glanced behind me. Still no sign of him. No doubt he was in one of the bedrooms or even the hall bathroom, either hooking up or shooting up. Either one killed me to think about. Finding it hard to stand up straight, I leaned against Axton. His blonde's eyes narrowed on me but I didn't pay her any mind.

"Liam invited you?" The tone of his voice told me I was going to get a lecture within the next few minutes and smiled at how protective he still was. We might not have been able to make things work, but he was still a good guy and wanted to protect me. Mostly from myself and the self-inflicted pain I caused when it came to Liam Bryant.

"*Si*, he invited me." I cleared my throat, realizing that my accent was becoming more pronounced. "So, here I am."

"And where is he?" Axton demanded, those hazel eyes turning more brown than green as he watched me.

I shrugged. "Who knows? Getting high. Getting his dick sucked. Could be either. Could be both." I clenched my jaw and wished for another drink. "Who cares?"

His eyes softened a little. "You okay?"

"I'm fine," I lied and turned back to the brick wall watching me just as close as Axton was. "Introduce me to your friends."

Ax blew out a long breath before finally making the introductions. "Brie, this is Dallas...my girlfriend. And the dude with the scary face is her muscle, Linc Spencer."

I spared Dallas a glance and a small smile before lifting my gaze back to Linc. Licking my lips, I took a step closer. Dallas stepped in front of me, though, as if she were the one protecting him. "You don't want to go there, girl. He bats for the other team."

I blinked as her words spoken in that southern twang registered with my intoxicated brain. "Excuse me?" No way she had just suggested that Linc was gay. No. Way. He was just... No. I couldn't accept that. He didn't act gay, didn't dress gay, nothing.

She didn't even bat an eye. "Trust me. Gay as they come."

Well, fuck.

A few minutes later some guy that was definitely gay came up to talk to Linc and I decided it was the best time to get another drink. First, however, I really needed a bathroom. I tried the one in the hall, but it was occupied. Muttering a curse, I decided on the one in the guest room, but of course the door to the bedroom was locked too. Judging from the noises coming from inside—and the way some chick was screaming for Brad to fuck her harder—I figured Axton needed to invest in a new mattress.

Rolling my eyes, I realized that I had one of two choices. Wait for the hall bathroom to open up—not really an option with how badly my bladder was screaming at me—or risk Axton's private bathroom in his bedroom. I'd really wanted to avoid that room because I was pretty sure that Liam was in there with one of his coke buddies from earlier.

Cursing my bladder, I turned in the direction of Axton's room. When I opened the door, I kept my eyes shut, not wanting to damage the rest of my heart and yeah, the last little bit of my soul as well. When I closed the door behind me and didn't hear anything, I slowly lifted my lids and breathed a sigh of relief when I found the room empty.

I quickly used the bathroom and washed my hands. While I stood there drying them, I glanced at myself in the mirror. I was still drunk, but it was starting to fade to a really good buzz. My cheeks were slightly flushed from the alcohol, my eyes glassy. I needed to retouch my lipstick, but I didn't bother with it. It wasn't like I was trying to impress anyone now. The guy I wanted—the guy I was starting to realize was the only guy I would ever really want—was doing things I didn't even want to think about.

Even though I wanted to move on and forget about Liam Bryant, I knew that wasn't going to happen. I could have slept with a hundred different guys and none of them would erase Liam from my heart. I mean, really, if sex for two years with Axton Cage hadn't driven Liam from my mind, it was pretty likely no one could. Pushing a few strands of hair back from my face, I tossed the hand towel on the sink and opened the door to the bedroom.

"I was starting to think I would never get you alone tonight."

My head snapped up and my breath caught in my lungs when I saw Liam leaning against the closed bedroom door. He looked so relaxed standing there, his arms crossed over his lean chest and a half smile on his beautifully masculine face. His eyes were what stopped me in my tracks, though. Those blue orbs were full of something predatory and exciting.

Mentally telling my heart to stop beating my chest to death, I lifted a brow at the rocker. "Oh, yeah? And why would you want to get me alone, Liam?"

The half-smile turned into a full-on grin as he pushed away from the wall and took two steps in my direction. "The usual reasons a guy wants to be alone with a hot chick. He wants to talk to her. Kiss her. Put his dick deep inside of her."

That last part was crass and crude, but parts of my body didn't seem to care as my panties became soaked with a need only this guy had produced in me—and he hadn't ever touched me. *Ah, hell.*

Swallowing hard, I crossed my arms over my breasts to hide the fact that my nipples were hard as diamonds. "So, what you're saying is you want to fuck me." Even as the words left my mouth, my body was mentally jumping up and down in anticipation, while my brain and heart were debating if I should take him seriously.

If I were honest with myself, I really—*really*—wanted him to fuck me. Maybe then I would be able to move on. What I was feeling might even just be because I needed to fuck him out of my system. Perhaps the love I felt for him was just really strong infatuation and plain and simple curiosity. Meanwhile, part of me knew that it was just wishful thinking. What I felt couldn't be fucked away.

I guess the real question I needed to be asking myself was whether or not I would survive a one-time fuck. Could I handle sleeping with Liam tonight and having him walk away from me the next day? Because that was how it was going to be. Liam Bryant didn't fuck the same girl twice, at least not in the few years that I'd known him. He was almost as bad as Shane Stevenson, manwhore extraordinaire. Almost.

While I was inwardly arguing with myself, Liam had crossed the room. His warm fingers touching my face and lifting my chin, urging me to look at him, snapped me out of my daze. I met his blue gaze and every argument that I'd just been having left my head.

The feel of his skin touching mine, the way his eyes seemed to be eating me up, made my body catch fire. When he lowered his head I didn't try to stop his kiss, but lifted onto my tiptoes to meet him halfway. The first brush of his lips over mine was like being electrocuted. My entire body felt like it was being zapped with something fierce from the inside out and I grasped his shoulders to steady myself.

His hands lowered to cup my ass, pulling me against him roughly. The feel of his erection against my lower stomach made me moan with pleasure. *Yes*, I silently cried. *Yes, this is what I've always wanted. What I've needed from the very second I bumped into him.* His hold on my ass tightened and I instinctively wrapped my legs around his waist when he deepened the kiss.

I licked his bottom lip, silently begging him to open up for me. I wanted to taste him. He growled and opened his mouth, offering me full access. The first brush of my tongue over his caused my senses to explode from the taste. It was slightly bitter, probably from all the drugs he'd been doing earlier, but there was something stronger underneath. Something far more powerful than any drug. It made my body seem to come alive for the first time in all my existence. Nothing had ever been as awe-producing for me as kissing this man.

Questing fingers lifted the skirt of my dress until they found my thong. I barely noticed when he wrapped his fingers around the left side and gave a hard tug. I'd only realized that he'd ripped my underwear off when I felt cool air touching my drenched pussy. Lifting my head, I watched as he tossed the ruined thong over his shoulder seconds before he lowered me to the bed.

"Fuck, you're so wet," he muttered when he cupped my aching pussy. "Why did I wait this long?" he asked and I realized he was talking to himself. "I've wanted you so damn long, little Brie. So damn long."

His confession only made me that much wetter and all I could think about was getting him deep inside of me. I reached for his belt and nearly broke a nail in my haste to get it undone. Liam bit out a curse as he just as impatiently tried to get my dress off of me. "I want you naked. I want to see every inch of you."

"Yes," I whispered fiercely and gave a small victory cry when his belt came undone and I reached for the snap of his jeans.

He was still struggling with the dress and I pushed him away, wanting to be just as naked as he wanted me. I reached for the zipper just under my right arm and pulled the dress over my head. The dress hadn't permitted a bra so I was left completely naked for him.

While I was undressing, I'd hoped he would have been too. Instead, he just stood there, his gaze scorching over every inch of my body as he seemed to engrave the sight of me like that into his memory. That thought made me bold and I spread my legs wide, touching myself as I opened the lips of my pussy to his gaze. I skimmed my middle finger over my clit and bit back a whimper.

The muscles in his neck worked as he swallowed hard. He rubbed one hand over his mouth before licking his lips. "I want to eat you up, little Brie. I want to lick that pretty pussy until I've swallowed every drop of your sweet essence."

His words produced another rush of wetness and when he watched the liquid desire coat my thighs, he growled something unintelligible and completely animalistic before dropping to his knees and burying his face in my pulsing, hot pussy. His tongue swiped over my clit and my hips reared off the bed at the pleasure.

Nothing had ever felt so good. No one had ever produced such a response from me. This was pure nirvana and I knew then and there that this wasn't going to be enough. One night was not going to burn him out of my heart. He was going to make me just as much an addict for him as he was an addict for drugs.

I didn't care.

My fingers thrust into his hair, holding him against me as he thrust his tongue inside my opening. He'd barely started yet I was hanging on by a thread. When he sucked my clit into his hot mouth, it was over. I cried his name and bucked against his face as the strongest orgasm I'd ever experienced raked my body.

Before I could come down off the high he'd just given me, I heard the sound of foil ripping and opened my eyes in time to watch him finish rolling the condom down his amazing cock. Oh, fuck, it was a great-looking cock. I wasn't going to compare him to any lover I'd ever had before, but he was definitely the thickest I'd ever had if not the longest. I swallowed back my brief fear that he would tear me when he thrust inside of me with that monstrous dick, and opened for him as wide as I possibly could.

His movements were jerky and I bit my lip as I prepared myself for him to enter me roughly. Yet, he didn't. He bent to kiss my lips softly while he guided his thickness to my opening and entered me so carefully that it made my eyes sting with tears. He eased into me slowly until he was as far as he could go. My flesh felt stretched to the point of almost pain, but oddly enough I loved it. Every nerve deep inside of me was hugging his thickness, my walls clenching around him as if begging him to go deeper.

He gently pulled out and slid back in just as slowly as the first time. My back arched and I saw stars. Damn, that felt good. So good. My hands slid under the shirt he hadn't bothered to take off and my nails dug into his sides as he thrust into me again, just as gently. I realized he was trying to be careful with me, that he was fighting back his need to fuck me hard, and my heart melted a little more. Somehow I knew that Liam didn't do this with other chicks. This was different for him.

Maybe I was special to him.

"You okay?" he asked, panting hard as he gritted his teeth and thrust slowly into me again.

"I'm good," I assured him and dug my nails a little deeper when he slid over a particularly sensitive part. "You feel so good, Liam."

"Ah, fuck, Brie. So do you." He kissed my neck then moved down to my breasts. When he sucked one nipple deep into his mouth and thrust just a little harder, I nearly exploded then and there. He lifted his head, as if sensing how close I was, and didn't want me to come yet. "You're so tight, babe. It's taking everything I have not to fuck you hard. But you're so small, I don't want to hurt you."

One more thrust and he rolled us so that he was on his back and I was over him. I pushed myself up so that I was sitting upright and tightened my thighs at his sides. He went an inch deeper inside me and I couldn't contain my small moan. Strong hands gripped my hips, urging me to move. I had adjusted to him now and slid up and down his thick cock with ease.

Pressing my hands against his flat stomach to steady myself, I rode his cock faster. His fingers tightened on my hips to the point of pain and I knew that I was going to be bruised in the morning. The thought made me smile and I rode him faster, needing him to lose control for me as much as I needed to come again.

"Keep...that up...and I'm...not gonna last," he bit out. "Fuck, woman. Ah, fuck."

I felt him growing harder and knew that he was going to erupt soon. I lifted a hand and touched my clit, rubbing hard quick circles as I rode Liam harder. "Liam," I moaned, so close to the edge but unable to fall over. I was waiting for him to come first, wanting to watch his face as I brought him the release we both needed so desperately. "Please. Come for me, Liam."

As if my plea was his trigger, he stiffened underneath me before shudder after shudder raked his body. His hips bucked against me, driving his thickness deeper. It was the look on his face that pushed me over, however. The sheer beauty of his face as his eyes darkened and then closed, the way his face tightened and his nose flared ever so slightly. His mouth opened in a silent scream as his lips formed my name.

Everything inside of me tightened and then contracted. My release this time was twice as hard as the first one he'd given me earlier. I fell forward, burying my face in his chest as my inner walls convulsed around his hardness. I closed my eyes as the force of my release became almost unbearable and I whispered his name over and over again.

Chapter Ten

Gabriella

FOUR YEARS EARLIER

I wasn't sure how much time passed before Liam shifted underneath me. I lifted my head and opened my eyes, watching him stretch like the feral beast that he was.

Had that really just happened? Had I really just had sex with Liam Bryant?

The fact that he was still inside of me attested to the answer, yet it still felt surreal.

"Fuck, Brie. That was mind-blowing." His voice was low, a little growly and full of satisfaction. Long, thick fingers traced circles on my hip and I nearly melted against him again.

I grinned down at him. "Yes, it definitely was. Why did we wait so long to do it?"

"Stupid, I guess." He wrapped his hands around my waist and sat up without dislodging himself from my body. I grasped his shoulders to steady myself when he buried his face between my breasts. "Damn, you smell good." I could feel him growing hard inside of me and felt my pussy rush with liquid desire in welcome.

A firm fist against the bedroom door had us both stiffening and Liam lifted his head to glare at the door. "What?" he yelled.

"Get your fucking clothes on, Liam," Axton called out. "I want these people out of my house in the next hour. I'm exhausted, man."

"Whatever, Ax." Liam slapped his hands against my ass, making me yelp in surprise. "Guess we're through here, little Brie." He kissed my lips quick and hard before lifting me off his lap and tossing me onto the bed.

Frowning, I watched as he stood, pulling off the condom before going into the bathroom. I heard the toilet flush and then the water turn on as he washed his hands. Was that it? It was over?

My chest clenched but my brain was mentally chastising me for thinking that this was more than a one-time thing. I might have been half drunk when this thing started, but that wasn't an excuse to be stupid. Liam wasn't the kind of guy to fuck the same girl more than once.

Fighting tears, I got jerkily to my feet and found my ruined panties. I was zipping up my dress when Liam came out of the bathroom. I didn't dare look at him or I might have done something stupid. Like cry. If he saw my tears, my shame would have been complete.

I searched the room and finally found my shoes just as Liam was pulling up his jeans. I didn't bother putting them on, couldn't risk taking the time. I could feel his eyes on me, burning me as he watched me move around the room. He didn't say a word and for that I was glad. I didn't want the whole 'thanks for a good time' speech from him. It would have made everything that much worse and I wasn't sure if I would have broken down crying or scratched his beautifully masculine face.

I crossed the room and opened the door without a backward glance. When I stepped through the door, slamming the heavy wood behind me, I nearly ran into the man standing on the other side. Lifting my eyes, I met Axton's hazel eyes and finally let a tear fall.

He blew out a long sigh and I lowered my head, unable to meet his gaze. For a long moment he stood there, watching me and I mentally prepared myself for the scolding I deserved. Fuck, I was so pathetic.

"How about another drink?"

My head lifted in surprise and I met Axton's kind eyes. "Ax…"

"Tequila... No. Whiskey. Yeah, that's what you really need right now." He smiled and grasped my arm gently, pulling me with him as he turned back toward the party. "That sound good to you?"

Another tear fell down my cheek and I hurriedly scrubbed it away as we stepped into the living room. "Yeah, Ax. Whiskey sounds really good right now."

Axton stayed with me while I drank two glasses of whiskey in the kitchen. He probably shouldn't have stuck around that long, not when his girlfriend was running around the apartment. He might have stayed with me for another glass but he heard Dallas laughing and excused himself.

I poured myself another glass and swallowed most of it before refilling it. Wondering what had caused Axton to look so stone-faced when he'd left me, I went back into the living room. It wasn't hard to find him. I saw the gay meathead, Linc, with Dallas and the guy who had approached him earlier. They were standing with Axton and Liam.

From where I was standing, it looked like Liam was eye-fucking Dallas. No wonder Axton had rushed off to check on his girl. I didn't know how serious the blonde was with Axton, but if she was like most of the chicks he dealt with, I wouldn't have been surprised if she had dumped one rocker for another.

Clenching my jaw, I turned away from the sight of Liam standing next to the beautiful blonde and nearly ran into a Demon for the second time that night. Drake didn't bother to try to steady me this time and I realized quickly that it was because he probably couldn't. The guy was seriously wasted and from the look on his face I kind of felt sorry for him.

"Dude, you need to go home." I pulled the nearly empty bottle of Jack Daniels from his hand and set it on the table beside him. My buzz was stronger now, which probably explained why I was being so nice to him, but I couldn't stand the look in his blue-gray eyes. He looked so lost, so broken.

"Lana's gonna be pissed when she sees me," he muttered and I figured he was talking to himself rather than me. "Em's gonna kick my ass." *Em's gonna tick my asp.*

His mutilation of the sentence made me giggle and I took his hand. "Yeah, Demon. She probably will tick that asp of yours." Shaking my head, I pulled him toward the door. "Where do you live, big guy?"

He mumbled his address as we stepped into the elevator and I repeated it to myself so I wouldn't forget. From the way he was swaying and was kind of hunched over, I figured getting the details out of him again was going to take a small miracle.

Downstairs, I asked the doorman to get us a cab and with the guy's help was able to get Drake into the back of one. The drive to his apartment didn't take long and I was hoping I could just let him out and the doorman would help him up to his room.

Wrong.

There was no doorman, just a guy manning the desk inside the building. He didn't look like he was going to be much help so I pushed Drake onto the elevator and asked him what floor. I barely heard him as he slumped against the elevator wall. Sighing, I punched the button for the right floor—I hoped—and closed my eyes as the feeling of flying took over on the quick trip up.

When the doors opened, it took me a minute to realize why the elevator had stopped. Those four glasses of whiskey had caught up to me and I was fighting my way through a haze of drunkenness. The doors almost closed before I moved, forcing them back once more.

"Drake," I grumbled.

"What?" He grunted, lifting his head from his chest where he had been half asleep.

"Let's go, dude." I waited for him to push himself away from the wall, sway a few times, and stumble off the elevator.

When he stopped in front of the apartment that I assumed was his, I waited for him to unlock the door. He just stood there, though, and I groaned. Realizing I'd have to do it myself, I started patting his pockets in search of a key and had to stick my hands in his front right jeans' pocket to pull out the key ring.

Once the door was unlocked and open, I had to help him to his room. He started pulling off his clothes the second that he was near his bed. I let him go, suddenly needing the bathroom.

Sitting down on the toilet, I let out a small moan in pleasure as I relieved myself. Sometimes, something as simple as peeing was euphoric. I leaned my head against the wall beside the toilet and closed my eyes.

Just for a minute, I promised myself. Then I would go home. I just needed to rest...

I wasn't sure how long I sat there, but when I opened my eyes I couldn't actually see anything. Groaning, I cleaned up and went to wash my hands. Where was I? Not home, that much I was sure of.

Yawning, I pulled off my dress and realized I wasn't wearing any panties. Oh yeah. Liam had destroyed them.

Bed. All I wanted was bed.

Opening the door, I found the bedroom dark and stumbled my way to the bed. My shin connected with the bedframe and I fell across the mattress with a curse.

"Angel?" a gruff voice muttered. "Come to bed."

Sighing, I straightened on the bed beside him and he pulled me against him. "Angel," he sighed almost contentedly.

Without realizing it, my eyes drifted shut and I was asleep instantly.

I woke with the sun shining through the bedroom window. As soon as I opened my eyes, my head protested and I snapped my eyes closed once again.

Fuck, I hadn't had a hangover like this in years. What had I drunk?

Moaning, I covered my face with my hands and slowly peeked through my fingers, trying to take in my surroundings.

Beside me, someone groaned and I moved my head slowly to see who I was lying next to. When I got a look at his face, I nearly threw up then and there.

Oh fuck. Oh shit. Oh… Fucking motherfucker. What the hell have I done?

Quickly, I tried to remember what had happened the night before.

Text from Liam. Party at Axton's. Sex with Liam. Mind-blowing, heart-breaking, amazing sex with Liam. Axton ruining the moment. Liam saying the fun was over. More drinking. Helping the Demon home. Climbing into bed with him.

The flashes I got of the night before helped me relax. No sex, thank God.

No, I didn't have to worry about the shit hitting the fan in that regard, but I still needed to get the hell out of there, and fast. I got out of bed as quickly as my queasy stomach and pounding head would allow. Getting to my feet was a challenge all on its own. I was dizzy and the world felt like it was trying to tilt me off into outer space.

It took a good five minutes to get to the bathroom where I emptied everything in my stomach into the toilet. Needing to clean up, I turned on the shower and stepped under the hot stream, scrubbing my body until my skin felt raw and abused. Okay. I was okay. I'd just get dressed and go home.

Wrapping a towel around myself, I picked up my dress—wait, where were my panties? Oh yeah. Sex with Liam. My mind shut down for a second as flashes of us fucking on Axton's bed last night filled my mind. Groaning, I went into the bedroom. As soon as I opened the door, I realized I should have dressed in the bathroom. The Demon was awake and as soon as he saw me, he jumped out of bed.

"What the fuck are you doing here?" He seethed.

I grimaced at his loudness. "Dude, down an octave, please. Some of us aren't used to raging hangovers like the pro you are." I touched a hand to my head where little men with jackhammers were bouncing on my brain. Fuck, that hurts.

"Did we..?" Drake asked, his voice quieter now.

"No," I assured him. "No sex."

"Fuck." I watched as his eyes glazed over with what could only have been tears. Yeah, I knew how he felt. I'd nearly cried with relief when I realized we hadn't screwed like rabbits too.

"Get your fucking clothes on and get out," he suddenly bellowed.

Those damn little men were having a wonderful time using my brain for a bouncy castle once again. "Trust me, Demon, I was doing just that. I'm not exactly proud of myself, you know." I dropped my towel, not embarrassed of my body in the least, and pulled on my dress while he pulled on a pair of boxers.

Opening the door, I stepped into the hall and he followed me into the living room...

As soon as I saw the three people already there, I realized I was in trouble. I glanced from the big, bald Demon to the beautiful chick who was his wife, and then to the redheaded little bitch sitting on a chair. Her big green eyes were full of fire and ice and I swallowed hard, knowing I wasn't going to walk out the front door without blood getting spilled.

Fuck.

Chapter Eleven

Liam

A change in the *beep-beep-beeping* pulled me from a restless doze. Jerking my head up, I glanced at the heart monitor over Gabriella's bed through blurry eyes. She didn't seem to be having a problem, although her heart rate had increased slightly.

That had to be a good thing. Her heart was getting stronger if it was beating a little faster.

Right?

Scrubbing a hand over my eyes to clear them of the dry tears that had made my lashes tangle together, I stood to relieve some of the pain in my leg. I needed some ibuprofen and a strong cup of coffee, and probably something to eat, too. I wasn't hungry, but I knew if I didn't eat something I wasn't going to be any good to Gabriella when she opened her eyes.

Yet, I couldn't bring myself to leave that little room. I didn't want to leave her alone back here. Sure, there were nurses, but they were just watching behind their desk or dealing with other patients. I didn't want Gabriella to open her eyes, not recognize where she was and be scared. If I left, they might not let me come back in and stay like they had for the last few hours. I'd have to stay in the waiting room with everyone else until appropriate visiting hours.

Shaking my head, because I wasn't going to chance that, I sat back down and linked my fingers through Gabriella's. Leaning forward, I rested my head on the bed again and brushed my lips over her fingertips over and over again. For some reason that had always soothed her in the past. When I'd moved into her apartment I'd do this every night to get her to fall asleep.

She would lie across the bed, needing room because she did a lot of moving around in her sleep. The first night I'd slept in the same bed with her she'd kicked me more than once and I'd woken up the next morning with a black eye. Since then she'd started sleeping an arm's length away.

I couldn't sleep without touching her, though. Not now. I would link our fingers together and brush my lips over each tip, not trying to be sexual about it, just needing the contact. Her sensual mouth would fall open ever so slightly and the softest sigh would leave her lips as her eyes would drift closed. Only when I knew she was resting peacefully would I find my own eyes drifting closed...

A firm hand on my shoulder forced my eyes open and I sat up and realized that Dr. Schiller was standing beside me. "What is it?"

Schiller gave my shoulder another firm squeeze before stepping back. "I need you to step out while we remove the breathing tube. She's breathing easier and showing signs that she might wake up soon. Waking up with a tube down her throat isn't something that you want her to experience."

Some of the panic that had been swallowing me up started to ease. "That's a good thing, though, right? She's going to be okay if she's breathing on her own, right?"

Another grim smile from the doctor. "It has given us better odds, Mr. Bryant." He glanced over at the bed. "She's a fighter, that much is for sure. And I think having you in here with her has helped considerably. As soon as we have her sorted, I'll have the nurse bring you back in. Grab yourself some breakfast."

"Breakfast?" I glanced down at my watch and realized it was six in the morning. I'd been back here since around two in the afternoon the day before. Had I slept that long? It sure as hell didn't feel like it. I was exhausted and stiff, in more pain than I normally was and knew that I was going to have to do something about it or risk the cravings for something other than the shit my orthopedic doctor prescribed.

"Shouldn't be longer than an hour before we bring you back, Mr. Bryant. Take care of yourself during that time. Your family is all still in the waiting room." The doctor nudged me toward the door with another squeeze to my shoulder and I reluctantly left.

Opening the door to the waiting room, I saw that the doctor was right. Nearly everyone was still there. Annabelle. Wroth and Marissa. Alexis and Jared, but not Jordan or Vince Sheppard. Emmie and Dallas. They were all resting—well, as much as anyone could rest in a waiting room. Most of them were asleep, while others just sat with their eyes closed, trying to rest.

It was Dallas I was relieved to see more than any of the others. I limped my way over to where she was sitting with her head leaned against a window, her blue eyes closed as she tried to sleep. She looked peaceful and I hated bothering her. She was pregnant, away from her husband and son. She should have been back at her bus, sleeping in a real bed. Instead, she'd been here with me since we'd brought Gabriella in two nights before.

I touched her shoulder and her eyes snapped open. I might hate bothering her, but I needed her right then. She was the only one who could help me. "Hey," she muttered in a voice hoarse with sleep. "She okay?"

I nodded. "Doc's back there with her. She is showing signs of breathing easier and might wake up soon. They're removing the tube."

Her eyes widened and a small smile lifted her lips. "That's a good thing, Liam."

"Yeah." I gripped my leg as I eased myself down beside her.

She watched me closely, those blue eyes narrowing when she saw the way I was holding my leg and gritting my teeth. "Is it bad?"

"Worse than I've had in a while," I told her and bent in half as I sucked in a deep breath, trying to fight through the pain. I didn't have pain like this very often these days. With daily exercise, anti-inflammatories, and a few other lifestyle changes, I'd been able to manage my pain. But I'd been sitting in the same position for too long with no physical activity at all and no anti-inflammatories at all in nearly forty-eight hours.

I was in agony.

"Okay, buddy. Let me see what I can do." Dallas stood. "I'm going to assume you don't want anything that's going to knock you out."

"Just something that will dull this a little, D. That's all I need." That was all I would ever chance putting into my body. I didn't dare put temptation in my path right then. Not when the cravings were already bad from the stress of everything else going on.

"I'll be right back," she promised and I nodded.

When she returned, she had another nurse with her who was carrying a syringe and a bottle of some kind of injectable medication. "This is some naproxen, Liam." Dallas told me as she took the needle from the nurse. "It's a pain medication with an anti-inflammatory. It's going to help ease some of the pain. I can give you another dose in four hours."

I nodded. I knew what naproxen was. I'd had it a lot a few months after my accident to help manage my pain. I'd stopped taking the stronger stuff as soon as I could manage it, terrified that I would be too tempted to start abusing them if I didn't. Having Dallas as my nurse back then had helped. She'd been in control of my medication intake and had helped me stay clear-headed enough not to go down that road.

"I know this sounds stupid, but I'm going to talk to Emmie about getting a treadmill in here. Maybe if you could walk a little it will help your pain a little more." Dallas cleaned a spot on my upper arm with an alcohol swab and then carefully stuck the needle in. I barely felt it and didn't grimace at the slight burn from the medication going in. When she was done she wiped the small spot again and put a Band-Aid over it.

Standing, she gave the used needle and other supplies to the nurse and thanked her. The other woman gave her a small nod and left without another word. I leaned back in the chair and closed my eyes as I waited for the naproxen to do its job.

"I'm going to get us something to eat," Dallas muttered. "Just sit tight while I go down to the cafeteria."

My eyes snapped open. "No, Dallas. You can't go alone. The paps are probably crawling around downstairs and who knows what other kinds of crazies are trying to get up here."

"It's okay, Liam. Seller's men are everywhere. I'll be fine." She gave me a small smile and pulled her shirt over the small baby-bump.

Seeing that little bump made my throat tighten as I remembered holding her son for the first time. I could honestly say that Dallas Cage was my best friend. She had been there for me through so fucking much and I would always love and respect her for that. This woman had my loyalty and allegiance for the rest of my life.

"Just be careful."

"I will. Now rest. I'll be right back."

The door closed behind her and I glanced around at the others spread around the room. Marissa and Wroth were still asleep, as was Alexis, although Jared wasn't. He had his arm around his wife, stroking his fingers over her long dark hair as he stared down at the screen of his phone.

Annabelle was awake now, too, and had her phone out as well. From the look on her face I knew that I should keep my distance for the moment, though. I might not have seen her in over seventeen years, but I remembered her well enough to know when not to mess with her.

Shaking my head, I turned my attention to Emmie. She was sitting all alone in the other corner of the room. She had her eyes closed, but I knew instinctively that she wasn't asleep. Her face was tense, pale with dark shadows under her eyes. I couldn't ever remember seeing Emmie look this bad before and wondered if she had gotten any sleep at all.

Standing slowly, I limped over to where she sat and dropped down beside her. She didn't open her eyes but I knew she was aware I was beside her. I sat there quietly for a few minutes before finally speaking. "How's Mia?"

A shuddery breath left Emmie's mouth and she opened her eyes. "Jesse says she's okay. She's still shaken up, though." Her voice was low, quiet, and full of a mixture of emotions I couldn't easily decipher. Pain, fear, anger were only a few of them.

"You should go back to the buses and be with her. I'm sure she wants you right now."

Her green eyes filled with tears but they didn't spill over. She sucked in a deep breath and shook her head. "I'm needed here. I can't leave until I know she's okay."

I frowned. "Mia needs you more, Emmie. And I think maybe you need her just as much right now. Go and hug your little girl. Reassure yourself that she's safe."

"I can't right now, Liam," she whispered brokenly and I felt tears of my own sting my eyes at how lost she looked right then. It was hard to see someone as strong as Emmie Armstrong like that. She'd had to deal with a lot of fucked-up shit in her life, but this... Yeah, this was possibly the worst of them all.

Understanding—yet not completely understanding—I took her hand and gave it a gentle squeeze before releasing her. "Okay." She was scared, of what I wasn't sure I knew or would ever understand, but I understood fear and pain and she had plenty of that raging around inside of her.

Dallas came back twenty minutes later with takeout boxes from the cafeteria for everyone while a guard I vaguely remembered held two drink carriers full of coffee. The smell of bacon, sausage, eggs and French toast assaulted me as soon as the door opened and I realized I hadn't eaten anything since lunch the day Gabriella had been shot. Now that my pain was under control, I realized I was starving.

The smell of the food roused everyone else and soon we were all eating together. I told them what the doctor had told me and Alexis started crying with relief. I knew that the doctor had said that it only increased Gabriella's odds a little, but I knew that she was going to be okay.

She *had* to be okay.

Two hours had gone by and there was still no sign of a nurse or the doctor to let me back in with Gabriella. With each ticking of the clock, my anxiety grew. I alternated between pacing, sitting, muttering curses, and avoiding anyone who even looked like they wanted to comfort me.

The waiting room was filling up again. Natalie and Devlin were back, along with Zander. Drake was there as well as Shane, both without their wives. Every time one of the Stevenson brothers even looked like they were going to approach Emmie, she found something else to do that kept her out of the room. I noticed her actions even through my misery so I knew that everyone else had to be aware of it too. She wasn't in a good place and I couldn't blame her. Almost losing her daughter must have been a nightmare come to life.

Scrubbing my hands over my face, I stopped in front of one of the windows and glared down at the hordes of paparazzi in the parking lot. They had been camped out for the last two days and more of them arrived by the hour. Not just the usual trash-mag people, either. The attempted kidnapping of a baby rock princess and the shooting of a rising rock star had made national news. Major networks had some of their best correspondents out there.

Emmie and Annabelle, along with the local police and the FBI, had given a press conference the day before, but there hadn't been much to tell. From what the specialist who had talked to Mia had learned, they didn't have any leads. The truth was they had at least a thousand leads, but no way of culling them. The attack on Shane and Harper's bus, twice now, had suggested that it was someone from Shane's past because it had been so personal an attack. Given that he had been the biggest player in the rock world up until he'd met Harper, it could have literally been one of thousands of women who had done it.

At least they had narrowed the sex of the perpetrator down to female. Mia had been able to tell them that much. A woman with a funny mark on her chin was the description the Feds had given the paps yesterday. We'd watched the press conference on the waiting room's small television and I'd slowly felt like I was drowning at the thought of that bitch being responsible for taking the most important person in the world away from me.

Behind me the door opened and I turned in hopes it was the nurse to let me back in to see Gabriella. It wasn't and my heart dropped in disappointment, adding to my anxiety.

Dallas stood when Axton entered the room, wrapping her arms around her husband as Jesse and Nik came in. "Is Cannon okay?" she asked her husband.

"He's fine, babe. Kenzie is watching him with a few of the Alchemy guys keeping her company," he assured her before kissing her. "How are you?"

"Tired, but I'll be fine." She buried herself deeper against him. "I'm so glad you're here."

The door opened again but I knew from the way the room suddenly felt tense that it wasn't the nurse. Emmie stopped when she entered the room, her eyes wide and a deer-caught-in-the-headlights look on her face when she saw Nik had arrived. I watched as she swallowed hard and started to turn to leave.

Nik moved fast and caught his wife around the waist, forcing her to face him. "Emmie." His voice was full of emotion and I saw the tears he unashamedly let fall. "It's okay, Em. She's okay."

"Wh-why are you here?" Emmie demanded. "You should be with Mia and Jagger. They need you."

"They're sleeping, baby girl. Layla and Felicity are watching over them and I have the bus surrounded with Seller's men. You're the one that needs me right now, Em." She shook her head but he gave her a small shake, not to hurt her but to snap her out of her denial. "Yes, you do. It's okay. I swear to you, it's okay."

A cry that sounded like it was being ripped from her soul filled the room as she pushed away from Nik. "No," she sobbed. "It's not fucking okay! We nearly lost her and it's all *my* fault, Nik. S-she only wanted to watch you. If I'd given in, if I'd let her come with us, then none of this would have happened. Our baby would have been safe with us and some twisted bitch wouldn't have tried to take her from me."

Nik wrapped his arms around her again, one hand grasping the back of her head as he pulled her against him. His chest muffled her broken sobs and he murmured soothingly to her, "It wasn't your fault, Em. None of this is your fault."

"You should hate me," she whispered, but the room was so quiet that everyone heard her. "I h-hate me."

"No, baby girl. I could never hate you. There's nothing to hate you over. You didn't do anything wrong." He pressed his lips to her temple and I had to look away from the raw emotion on my friend's face. "Mia is safe, Em. She's safe, but she misses you. She thinks that you're mad at her. Please, sweetheart. Come back to the bus with me and talk to her."

He held her for a long while in silence as if letting her absorb his strength. No one seemed to even be breathing, the room was so quiet. After a few minutes Emmie finally nodded. "O-okay."

Tears were still pouring down her face as Nik linked their fingers together and pulled her from the room. Jesse, Drake, and Shane followed after them but the room remained quiet as the force of Emmie's pain remained behind, soaking into every one of us.

Chapter Rock Twelve

Gabriella

Tugging. Lots of uncomfortable tugging. A fiery shot of pain burned through my lungs. I tried to open my eyes to tell whoever was torturing me to go fuck themselves, but no matter how hard I willed my eyes to open, they refused to cooperate.

I inhaled in frustration only to realize that I couldn't really draw as much air as I needed. As if a sound was coming from far away, I heard something protesting, a machine maybe, before I felt something being shoved into my nose and cool air filling my sinus cavities a second before my burning need for oxygen was quenched.

The noisy machine instantly quieted and I sighed in relief.

Cool fingers prodded over my body, not in a sexual way, but definitely not in a way that made me comfortable. Everywhere the cool fingers touched it felt like I was being electrocuted with pain. What the hell was wrong with my chest? That was where those cool fingers kept prodding the most and it felt like whoever was touching me was slowly killing me from the pain they were producing.

Stop! I tried to speak but my lips wouldn't work and I ended up screaming the word in my head instead. *Please, please stop. It hurts so much.*

The more I tried to beg for the pain to end, the more it hurt. Panic mixed with the pain began to suffocate me. Why couldn't I speak or open my eyes? What was wrong with me? This was scary. Terrifying.

The fear was trying to drown me and I moved my mind away from the darkness that was threatening to swallow me up.

I don't want to be here. I don't want to be here. Please, God, I don't want to be here...

FOUR YEARS EARLIER

The ringing of the doorbell jerked me awake. Frowning at the clock beside my bed, I saw that it was just after two in the morning. Who the hell would come calling at that ungodly hour?

I continued to lie there, debating whether or not to get up and answer or just pretend to not be home and go back to sleep. Tough decision. Get out of my nice warm bed to face a possible serial killer or go back to dreamland.

Hmm. Killer or sleep?

My eyes started to drift closed and I was letting sleep consume me again when the doorbell rang again. My eyes snapped open and I tossed back my covers. Reaching for my robe, I pulled it on as I walked through my dark New York apartment. I was in the living room when the asshole—possible serial killer—rang the doorbell again.

"Who is it?" I called, but no one answered.

Glaring at the door, I wondered if a serial killer would actually use the doorbell. It was unlikely, but crazier things had happened. Blowing out a frustrated sigh, I moved to the front door and stood on tiptoes to see through the peephole. My eyes focused on the person on the other side of my door and I stepped back in a mixture of surprise and confusion.

What the hell was he doing here?

"Open the door, little Brie. I know you're in there," Liam's voice called out and I stepped back in shock.

I hadn't seen Liam in over a month. While I'd been getting my ass kicked by Layla Thornton and Emmie Armstrong, he'd been on a plane to Tennessee. Axton had said Marissa had called and Liam hadn't even hesitated to go home. It had only confirmed for me that our stolen moment in Axton's bedroom was all we were ever going to have. I'd have to accept that and live with it.

During the past month I'd tried to forget about him, but after tasting nirvana it was hard to contemplate anything else. I thought about him—about that night—all the time. Liam was constantly on my mind and it was slowly driving me insane. I wanted him again. I wanted him and so much more.

A fist pounded on the front door. "Come on, Brie. It's been a long night. Let me in."

I pushed my long, thick hair back from my face. "What do you want, Liam?" I demanded, still not sure if I was going to open the door or not.

"So many things and not one of them can be accomplished with this fucking door between us." His voice was full of sensual promise mixed with what could only be described as frustration. Goose bumps popped up along my entire body and I clenched my legs together in hopes of stopping the rush of liquid desire.

"Are you high?"

He chuckled. "Are you?"

I clenched my hands at my sides. Of course he was high. When wasn't he? Muttering a curse, I snapped on the lamp by the entrance and opened the door just enough so that I was half standing in the doorway. "What do you want, Liam?"

He stepped closer and I could see his eyes were glassy and bloodshot even in the dim lighting coming from the corridor light and the single light I'd snapped on before opening the door. "You," he murmured as his eyes skimmed over my body from head to toe and back again. "Fuck, I want you, little Brie. Let me in, baby."

The ache between my legs began to throb at his imploring tone and I clenched my thighs together harder. "I'm not interested," I lied. Yeah, I was going to hell for telling such a huge lie. "Go home and sleep whatever you're on off."

"I just flew from Nashville to New York to see you, Brie. And now you're just going to send me away?" His grin was predatory,

103

his eyes full of hunger. "I don't think so, little Brie. I plan on getting what I came for."

I lifted my brows at him, trying desperately not to let him see how his words were affecting me. He'd flown from Nashville just to see me? Was he out of his mind on drugs or had he been thinking about me just as much as I'd been thinking of him? Was I an obsession that was eating at his psyche like he was doing to me?

Liam lowered his head until his nose skimmed over the tip of mine. His breath was minty, telling me he'd recently brushed his teeth. I inhaled deeper and realized that he was wearing cologne as well. His clothes didn't look wrinkled, as they would have done if he'd just gotten off a plane.

"Did you go to Axton's?" I demanded.

"No way. I stopped at my hotel on the way over. Didn't want to show up looking like some damn homeless man." He lifted his hand to cup my neck, his thumb caressing over the pulse racing at the base of my throat. "Hell, Brie. You're so fucking beautiful. Let me in, sweetheart. I need to be with you."

I couldn't hide the shiver that his touch mixed with his provocative words produced. Without realizing it, I leaned toward him, silently offering myself to him. "Liam…" I moaned his name as his lips brushed over my cheek.

"Brie." He kissed down my jaw before sinking his teeth into the sensitive skin just under my ear. "I need you, Brie. Let me in before I explode." He ran his tongue over the small sting his teeth had left. "Please, baby? Please, let me in."

One big hand cupped between my legs, and I was helpless to hide the fact that I wasn't wearing panties underneath my thin nightgown—or that I was drenched with hot arousal. He sucked in a deep breath as a small whimper escaped me. "Fuck," he bit out and buried his head in my neck. "Let me in. Now."

I let go of the door and wrapped my arms around his neck, unable to fight what I was feeling a second longer. He shuddered as I started to kiss any part of his face I could reach. His hand left my pussy and wrapped around my waist, lifting me a few inches off the ground as he stepped into the apartment and slammed the door behind us as he moved farther inside.

The hardness of the door was cool through my thin robe and gown as he pushed me up against it. I wrapped my legs around his thighs even as he was struggling to undo his belt. I was starting to tremble with the force of my need and tried to help him. A growl escaped his delicious mouth seconds before he covered mine to distract me. I thrust my fingers into his hair, keeping him locked to me.

I was on fire. My body was one big throbbing ache as we devoured each other's mouths in a frantic fight for satisfaction. My body was going under in one wave after another of pure unchecked desire while my brain was trying to decipher if I was still sleeping or not. For weeks I'd been dreaming of this, of having him in my arms again, of losing myself in the soul-destroying passion that I'd only ever experienced once in my life—*with this man.*

Sharp teeth sank into the swell of my breast and I cried out in a mixture of pain and pleasure. It was just enough pain to make my stupid brain realize this was indeed real.

Liam pulled back and we were both struggling for air. I leaned my head back against the coolness of the door, watching him through half veiled eyes as he freed himself from his jeans and boxers and tore open a condom. His fingers were trembling as badly as my own were as he rolled it down over his thick tip. Once it was in place, he guided his amazing girth to my entrance.

Just as I'd expected the first time, I thought he would slam into me. But just like the first time, he stopped, gritted his teeth, and slowly eased himself inside of me. The slight burn of my inner muscles spoke of how much he stretched me and I welcomed the small discomfort as he eased himself inch-by-inch deep inside of me.

The tip touched my womb and he stopped, breathing hard as sweat beaded on his brow. Cursing viciously, he lowered his head until his face was buried between my breasts, sucking in deep breath after deep breath. Big hands tightened on my ass to the point that I knew I'd have bruises by morning, but I didn't care.

"Goddamn, Brie. You feel so fucking amazing." He slowly lifted his head. Blue eyes clashed with my own and I saw clearly just how overwhelmed he was from being inside of me. It was the same for me. "I've dreamed of this. Ever since I got a taste of you I haven't been able to think of anything else. You're like a fucking drug, and it's worse than any other addiction I've ever had. I can't..." He broke off and shook his head as he pulled out a few inches before thrusting back roughly. "I can't fight this anymore."

I didn't know what to say. His confession left me speechless. When he thrust again I couldn't have said anything even if my life depended on it. I was lost in the tidal waves of pleasure that were crashing over me. My inner walls started contracting as my pussy began to drip with the building flood of release that was about to drown me.

"Ah, God." He threw his head back. "I've barely started and I'm going to explode. Fucking hell, Brie. What are you doing to me?"

I opened my mouth but nothing came out except a keening cry that felt as if it was being stripped from my lungs. I was coming harder than I'd ever come in my life at the hands of the only man I'd ever loved. Yet, I despaired at the thought of the end. He was going to leave me again. In the morning I'd be alone again, with only more memories to haunt my dreams every night.

"Brie." Liam cried my name as his entire body stiffened. I tightened my legs around his hips, holding him deep inside of me while his body gave a powerful jerk as his release washed over him.

Warm, damp lips caressed over my face long after he was finished. I stroked my fingers through his short hair as our breathing started to even out, trying to keep the tears at bay. As soon as he lifted his head, he was going to leave me. I'd have to go back to my cold bed and try to find sleep. Alone.

Fuck, why did I feel so alone all of a sudden?

His head started to lift and I clenched my eyes closed in case I wasn't able to hide my pain from him. Strong fingers eased their hold on my ass, but he didn't pull from my body. He tucked me closer to his chest and turned away from the door. Surprised, I tried to look up at him but he only held me closer.

"Liam?" I murmured, confused.

"I'm exhausted, baby. Give me a few minutes and we can go for round two." He bent and laid me on my bed before straightening and pulling off his shoes and clothes. It took less than half a minute and then he was lying beside me, pulling the covers over the both of us.

I realized that my back fit perfectly against his front as he tucked my head under his chin. My surprise was slowly starting to fade, only to be replaced with contentment and I rubbed my bare ass against his thickness. He chuckled, cupped his hand between my legs and yawned. "I could get used to this."

So could I.

I could feel him drifting off to sleep, and then knew for sure when his breathing evened out and a slight snore escaped him. I bit my lip to keep from grinning. Yeah, I could definitely get used to this…

"Son of a bitch!"

I jerked awake at the harsh curse. It took me a moment to realize where I was and who was cursing at me. I blinked open my eyes to find Liam across the bed with his hand pressed to his eye. I frowned then looked down at myself.

I was tangled in the blankets and on the other side of the bed than where I'd been when I'd fallen asleep. Sighing, I gave him an apologetic grimace. "Did I kick you?"

His glare was starting to ease into a smirk and he nodded. "If you didn't want me to sleep with you, all you had to say was no, little Brie."

I pushed my tangled hair back from my face. "Sorry. I'm kind of a kicker." Okay, so that was the understatement of the century. I've always moved around in my sleep. Some people sleepwalk, but I tend to do all my exploring under the covers. My aunt had always teased me that I could teach kickboxing from my bed if I ever decided that music wasn't what I wanted.

From the way Liam was still holding his eye, I had to assume she was right.

"So, that wasn't your subtle way of telling me to get the hell out your apartment?" he murmured.

I tried to hide my shiver, but there was no hiding the fact that my nipples were diamond-hard underneath the thin material of my nightgown. "No," I assured him. "I kind of like you here."

Oh shut up, you dumb cow, a voice in the back of my head shouted. *Stop giving him ammunition to use against you later on.*

The smirk on his face turned softer, his eyes seeming almost gentle. "Yeah?"

"Yeah," I whispered, ignoring that damn voice trying to caution me against letting this rocker too close.

Liam moved so fast I didn't realize what he was doing until I was lying on my back underneath him. My legs spread of their own volition and he settled between them so perfectly it was almost like he was made specifically to be there. I felt his thick hardness nudging against my entrance and had to bite back a small mewl of pleasure.

Warm lips brushed over my eyes tenderly before he captured my lips in a kiss that had me arching against him in search of relief. "Tell me to shut up anytime, but I want to run something by you."

I blinked open my eyes when he lifted his head. "Um, okay."

He grinned. "I don't know if I'm going to be a good boyfriend or whatever, so I'm not going to put a label on this. But how would you feel about making this thing between us a regular occurrence?"

I was brain-dead. That had to explain it. Why else weren't his words making any sense to me? Licking my lips, I tried not to look hopeful as I spoke. "What do you mean by 'this thing'?"

It seemed like a good question to me, or at least a good start. His question could have any different number of meanings. Did he want to have regular late-night hookups? Would we be fuck-buddies whenever we were in the same city? Or—*oh fuck, the hope was choking me on this one*—or did he want something more?

His grin dimmed ever so slightly and I saw something I had never seen in Liam Bryant's eyes before. Vulnerability. "Us. Spending time together. Going to dinner and places. Sleeping in the same bed. Falling asleep together after having the most amazing sex I've ever had in my life… That kind of thing."

I bit the inside of my cheek to keep from answering him so quickly that it sounded desperate. Holy shit. Liam was really offering me what I'd been hoping for. He wanted more.

I lowered my eyes so he couldn't read my emotions as easily. "I might like that," I murmured. "But only if you aren't sticking your dick in other pussies."

His face tightened. "I can promise you that isn't going to happen. Can you promise the same?"

I lifted a brow. "I'm pretty sure I won't be dipping my dick in any pussies, so you're safe there."

His lips twitched, but he was able to fight back the grin I could see he wanted to let go. "Don't be a smartass, Brie. You know what I'm saying." He thrust his hips roughly against my opening, the tip of his thickness nudging my pussy lips apart but he didn't sink into me and I nearly cried out with the pain of not having him sinking deep inside my aching body. "I want to be the only fucker who gets to sink into this tight pussy. It's mine, little goddess."

I whimpered as the crown of his dick skimmed over my clit.

"Say it," he commanded in a voice tight with need. "Tell me that this pretty pussy is mine."

My eyes drifted closed as I tried to hold onto the sheer pleasure of having him touching me like that. "It's yours," I breathed. "All yours, Liam."

He kissed my neck, his teeth sinking into the tender flesh where my shoulder and neck met. "I want to be yours, little Brie."

Tears burned my eyes even as pleasure curled in my chest. I wanted that too. "Y-you do?"

"Yes. I've wanted it for so fucking long." He buried his face in my neck so I couldn't see him. "I wanted it when I came to New York last month. I thought I was never going to get you alone at that stupid party I threw at Axton's. Then I did and got so carried away that we ended up fucking each other's brains out and didn't get a chance to talk afterward. You left and I had to go back to Tennessee to help Rissa."

"You could have called me," I murmured.

"No, babe. I couldn't. I don't do that kind of shit. I don't even call my sister. I can barely stand to text." He brushed his lips over the shell of my ear, his heavy breath making goose bumps pop up over my entire body. My thighs opened even more for him, but he didn't do anything but kiss my neck again, even though I could feel how much he wanted me. He was holding himself back, as if he needed to talk this out before he could sink into my willing body again.

"I'm not a hearts-and-flowers kind of man, Brie. Romance isn't my thing. It never has been. I'm not ever going to be the guy you deserve because I'm a selfish bastard. But I want you so fucking much that I'm going to be even more selfish and ask you to be mine knowing that I can't give you those things." He skimmed his nose over the base of my throat and kissed across my collarbone. "Can I be yours, little Brie?"

He lifted his head and I shut my eyes quickly before he could read the emotion churning in them. If he'd seen my eyes right then he would have known that it didn't matter that he was a selfish bastard. I'd always known that and it hadn't stopped me from loving him. I'd fallen for this rocker knowing that he wasn't perfect, knowing that he came with a lot more heartache than most women could handle.

Good thing I wasn't most women.

I wanted him the way he was. Loved him the way he was. I didn't want to change him.

I only needed him.

"Yes," I whispered and felt him shudder against me.

Liam buried his face in my chest and stayed there for a long moment. When he finally lifted his head, his eyes were clearer than I'd ever seen them. He smiled and butterflies actually fluttered in my belly. "Thank fuck."

Chapter Thirteen

Gabriella

FOUR YEARS EARLIER

"Brie!"

I finished tightening the strap on my heel and straightened as the door to my bedroom opened. I slowly turned to find Liam standing in the doorway, trying to get his tie sorted. He had it in a knot, but it was definitely not the right kind of knot.

Laughing, I stepped forward and grasped the ends of the silky dark-red tie that matched my dress. "How did you do this?" I asked as I used my long nails to try to undo the knot he'd tightened in the material.

His eyes weren't on the tie, however, but on the cleavage that my dress was showing off. I lifted one hand and tapped him teasingly on the jaw, trying to get his attention off my breasts for the moment. He lifted his hungry gaze and I knew if I didn't distract him we weren't going to be leaving the apartment that night.

If tonight were anything but the biggest event in the music world, I would have taken him up on the unspoken promise in his blue eyes. Unfortunately for both our aching bodies, it was and we had to be there.

The song I'd collaborated with OtherWorld on, "Shatter Me", was being recognized and we were all receiving a special award for it at the Grammys. When I'd written that song, I'd only been thinking of the pain Alexis was going through at the time. I never expected it to become a kind of anthem for teens fighting depression, but more specifically the ones who had been self-harming. Over the last two years, my song had become part of support groups and recovery programs. Tonight, the fans and several national teen mental health organizations were handing over an honorary Grammy because of it.

For me, it was going to be my first Grammy; for OtherWorld, that was an entirely different story. They had been in this business for a hell of a lot longer than I had and had several to their name. This year they weren't up for any nominations but Demon's Wings was so we would have to see them there as well, but I wasn't going to let that bother me tonight.

I'd spent the entire day getting ready. I had on a dress that had been made specifically for tonight by an up-and-coming Italian designer that my aunt had recently taken on as a client. My stylist had spent hours working on my hair, makeup, and nails before leaving half an hour ago. So, no matter how much I wanted to take Liam up on his offer, there was no way I was going to let him muss me up.

"You look beautiful," he muttered as I finally worked the knot open and began to fix the disaster he'd made of the expensive tie. "How the fuck did I get so lucky?"

I bit the inside of my cheek and concentrated on the task at hand as butterflies fluttered in my stomach. I'd been asking myself the same thing for the last four months. How was it possible that I had this man—the man who I'd always dreamed of being mine—in my bed every night?

Liam might have said he wasn't going to label what we had as that of a boyfriend/girlfriend nature, but that was exactly what it was. No, I thought as I finished up the perfect knot and tightened it at his throat. It was more than that. Much more.

We were practically living together now. No matter where I was, he was always there too. He rarely went home to Tennessee and the few times he had, he'd asked me to go with him. The closet in my New York apartment was half full of his things, just as my West Hollywood apartment was. We'd never really talked about his moving in, it had just kind of happened.

With his tie finally in place, I kissed his lips, for once not having to stand on my tiptoes to do it with the heels I was wearing. I wanted to linger, deepen the kiss, but knew that I was tempting my beast with just the soft brush of my lips over his. Stepping back, I gave him a sassy smile and turned back to the bed for my purse.

Behind me I heard him muttering one vicious curse after another under his breath and I grinned. Facing him once more, I gave him a wink as I walked around him toward the door. "Let's go or we'll be late."

"I don't want to go," he grumbled as he followed me out of the apartment and into the elevator.

"It's going to be fun," I assured him. "Plus, this is for me as much as you and OtherWorld. Can't you grin and bear it for a little while? For me?" I gave him a small pout.

Large hands grasped my waist and pulled me against his lean body. I felt his lips against my hair as he blew out a long breath. "Yeah, I guess I can for you." He didn't sound happy about it, but that he was going to put up with what went with tonight—*for me*—had my heart melting just a little bit more for him.

I curled myself against him, hiding my smile as we rode the elevator down to the first floor. He might seem all moody, badass rocker on the outside, but I knew that he was all soft and cuddly on the inside. At least with the ones he cared about. I was beyond thrilled that I was included in that small number of people.

Outside, the doorman was already ready to open the door to the limo that was waiting on us. Liam's hand grasped my elbow as I went to step inside and I lifted my head in confusion. His face looked stormy and I didn't like when he got that look on his beautifully masculine face.

"What's wrong?" I murmured, aware of the others already in the limo. We were all arriving together and everyone else had already been picked up. Their laughter reached my ears and I realized at least one member of OtherWorld had already been drinking tonight. Probably Devlin and Zander from the way those two were howling like drunken idiots.

Releasing my elbow, Liam cupped my face and dropped a soft kiss on my lips. "You're with me tonight, okay? Not Ax. I know the media is going to assume that you and he are back together when you walk down the red carpet, but make sure you correct them when they ask if you two are back together."

I lowered my gaze so he wouldn't see my eyes and tried to get my heart under control. Over the last four months, Liam and I had tried to keep a low profile about our relationship. The few times we'd been spotted out together had been when we were out with the other members of his band. Each time there had been a picture in the trashy magazines speculating if I was back together with Axton Cage.

I'd ignored the magazines and hadn't bothered to comment when the paps would ask if I was dating Axton again. Until now, Liam hadn't wanted to go public about our relationship. That he was tonight of all nights, had my heart pounding with excitement.

"Okay?"

At the uncertainty in Liam's voice, I lifted my eyes to his and let him see the pleasure on my face. "Yeah, Liam. Okay."

He let out a relieved laugh and urged me into the back of the limo. As I slid across the bench seat to let him in, my eyes started to adjust to the dim lighting. Devlin and Zander were sitting on the bench seat directly across from us. Each had a tumbler of bourbon in their hands, their drink of choice. Devlin's long hair was down around his wide shoulders and his dark skin looked exotic matched with those mesmerizing aquamarine eyes. Zander looked sinful in his suit with his hair styled carelessly and his ink standing out on his hands.

On the bench seat to my left sat Wroth with Marissa and I gave her a warm smile when I met her blue gaze that was so much like her brother's. She looked beautiful in her ice-blue evening gown and her long glossy hair in soft waves falling to her waist. Marissa Bryant might possibly have been the most beautiful chick I'd ever set eyes on. She and her brother shared some of the same facial features that they had to have inherited from their father since they didn't share the same mother, but where Liam's were distinctively masculine, Marissa's were very feminine. It wasn't her exquisite looks that made Marissa so beautiful, however. It was her sweet, loving personality that shined through her eyes that bespoke her true beauty.

Beside her sat perhaps the scariest man on the planet. Wroth Niall was a broody motherfucker with a soft spot for only one person—Marissa. If his size didn't intimidate you, his rough voice surely would, but it was the look in his eyes that had always warned me to stay clear of this particular rocker. There was darkness in his eyes, and I didn't mean just their color. Wroth was ex-marine, a deadly weapon who had used his skills to survive a tour of active duty overseas. I was brave and didn't care who I ran my mouth to, but even I knew to stay clear of enraging that sleeping beast.

To my right, Axton was sitting by himself. As usual he was messing on his phone, texting away. I didn't need three guesses to know who he was talking to. Even when we had been trying to make a go of the disaster that had been our relationship, Axton hadn't been able to go more than a few hours without talking to Emmie in some shape or form. She would text him just as much and they had usually been random things that would make Ax laugh.

I frowned at him as he continued to type, wondering if it had been because of his need to constantly be in contact with Emmie that had ruined his relationship with that Dallas Bradshaw chick. He hadn't talked about it, especially not with me, but I couldn't help wondering what had happened to make them call it quits. I'd actually kind of liked her.

Liam's arm draped over the back of the seat and his fingers cupped around my shoulder, pulling me against his side and drawing my attention back to him. The doorman shut the door and moments later the driver pulled into traffic.

"You look beautiful, Brie." Marissa offered me a bottle of cold water and a kind smile. "You and Li look so good together."

Pleasure curled in my chest. "Thanks, Rissa. That dress is lovely on you. It makes your eyes sparkle."

"Yeah, Riss. You look beautiful," Liam told his sister, causing her cheeks to heat with pleasure. "Did Wroth take you shopping?"

"No." She shook her dark head. "I went with Emmie and Layla when I got into town two days ago. It was fun, and today they invited me over to get ready at Emmie's." She gave a delighted laugh. "I love hanging out with those two."

I gritted my teeth and tried to keep my smile in place. It wasn't Marissa's fault that I detested Emmie. Layla, I could just about stomach, but Emmie... Yeah, I wasn't going to open that can of worms tonight of all nights.

"Harper and Lana weren't there?" Axton asked.

"They didn't get in until last night, and had things to do, but they will be there tonight with Shane and Drake." Marissa took a sip from her own bottle of water. "I hope we all get to sit together. I would love to catch up with Harper."

"You will see her later at the after-parties," Liam assured his sister. "Did Dallas come?"

I saw Axton stiffen out of the corner of my eye. When Marissa shook her head, his shoulders seemed to droop for a moment before he straightened them and turned his attention back to his phone.

"No, she and Linc couldn't make it out for this. Dallas has school and Linc had to work."

I couldn't help the curiosity that filled me. "School?"

"Dallas is going to nursing school to be a registered nurse," Marissa informed me with excitement in her sweet voice. "She's always wanted to be a nurse and she's finally going to become one. Emmie and Layla said that Dallas is working her butt off to stay at the top of her class, but I know she's going to make an amazing nurse."

"I bet her mother just loves that," Axton muttered.

"Her mother?" I sat forward slightly, eating up all the details like I was watching some kind of soap opera or something. The way he'd said 'mother' told me that whatever relationship Dallas Bradshaw might have with the woman who had given birth to her wasn't a pretty one.

"Total bitch, that one." Axton didn't look up from his phone as he spoke. "Attention whore."

Zander snorted. "Tell us how you really feel, Ax."

"Take my mom and multiply by two," Axton grumbled and everyone around us sucked in a deep breath but didn't say anything more about the subject.

Of course my curiosity began to eat at me even more. I'd never met Axton's mother, or anyone else from his family for that matter. He never mentioned them and the one time I'd brought up the subject when we'd been together he'd just said the only family he needed or wanted was Emmie and the Demons.

The fact that he hadn't said OtherWorld had told me just how much of an outcast he still felt with his band-brothers. I'd felt bad for him. It had always been apparent to me that the other members of OtherWorld didn't include Axton in their lives outside of the band very often. The others were close in one way or another, but Axton was the outsider. All the stories of them growing up had never included Axton at all.

My brow still furrowed, I took a small sip of my water before offering the bottle to Liam. He took a thirsty swallow just as the limo slowed and moments later the door was opened by some skinny guy in a nice suit.

Wroth and Liam both held out their hands to help Marissa out before anyone else had even moved. I hid a smile as Liam took gentle care to assist his sister from the car and then climbed out behind her before offering me his hand. I wanted to stop and kiss him but, between the guys complaining to get out behind me and the skinny guy urging us to move forward, I wasn't able to.

Sighing, I turned and got my first look at what the red carpet at the Grammys was like. Cameras were flashing from all angles, fans and paps alike crying out to everyone who got out of a car. Entertainment television hostesses were stationed at various spots along the carpet leading into the Staples Center.

Picture after picture was snapped as we made our way down the red carpet. We were asked random questions like *Who are you wearing* or *Who do you think will win a Grammy in blah-blah genres*. No one asked if I was with Axton and I think Liam actually breathed a sigh of relief when we got to the last stop before entering the building.

As we were ushered toward the entrance, someone called out to Axton and I lifted my head to find Emmie in a gorgeous gray dress iced out in the most amazing diamond necklace I'd ever set eyes on walking toward our group. Axton stepped away and wrapped his arms around her before giving her a kiss on the cheek. I didn't hear what they were saying but she pulled him back down the red carpet where Drake Stevenson was standing with his wife and Cole Steel. I assumed it was for publicity for *America's Rocker* and dismissed Axton from my mind as we were ushered to our seats.

Over the next hour, the chairs around us filled up. Axton sat a few seats behind us with Drake, Lana, and Cole with the other Demons and their wives/girlfriends to our left. People stopped to speak to us and at one point Wroth escorted Marissa to the ladies room. We were pretty close to the stage and I was starting to get a little nervous.

As if sensing my anxiety, Liam caught hold of my hand and gave it a little squeeze just as the lights were dimmed and the award show began. "Relax, little Brie. I'm going to be right here beside you all night."

I gave him a small smile and bit the inside of my cheek to keep from uttering the words that were almost choking me tonight. I hadn't dared tell him that I loved him yet. Who knew how he would react if I told him right then? Our relationship was perfect at the moment and there was no way I was going to risk fucking it up by saying three little words that packed the power of a category-five hurricane.

I was exhausted after the Grammys, but apparently we still had several more hours to go before I could even dare go home. After-parties were where all the big deals were made in the rock world. I hated them, but knew I had to grin and bear it for at least a little while longer.

Sighing, I lifted my glass of champagne to my lips and took a small sip as I glanced around the extravagant home of some big-shot record label exec. I didn't remember the guy's name and really didn't care, but I did know that refusing to show up at the dude's party could make or break someone's career. Of course, the OtherWorld guys knew him.

The little enthusiasm I'd had for this party vanished the second that Emmie and her Demons showed up. They had won the Grammy for Best Rock Single and were ready to party. I'd excused myself and gone to the bathroom when the other rockers and their wives/girlfriends—minus Drake and Lana—had come over to shake hands with the OtherWorld guys. When I'd come back, everyone had been spread around the room and I hadn't been able to find Liam.

Figuring he'd been off with friends he knew, I'd grabbed a glass of really good champagne from a passing waiter and found a corner to people-watch from. That had been half an hour ago and I was on my second glass of champagne. I didn't know where Liam was and hadn't seen anyone else from our group in that time.

Pulling my phone from my clutch, I found I didn't have any texts from Liam letting me know where he was, and I grimaced. Muttering a curse under my breath, I tossed back the rest of the contents in my glass and exchanged the empty glass for a fresh one.

"Maybe you should try something a little stronger."

I lifted my head to find Axton walking toward me. There was a grim smile on his face and two tumblers of some kind of amber liquid in each hand. Swallowing the rest of my fourth glass of champagne, I set the empty glass on a small table and readily took the offered liquor from Axton.

Taking a cautious sip, I realized that it was a well-aged whisky and smiled my thanks as I took a bigger swallow.

"Saw the bottle of Macallan and thought of you," Axton muttered as he took a swallow from his own glass. "I hope Petrova doesn't get pissed that I opened his 1945 bottle."

I coughed and nearly spit the whisky out through my nose. Axton's hand slapped me on the back roughly several times before I could breathe again. When I could, I glared up at him. "You...opened a 1945 bottle...of Macallan?" I wheezed.

He shrugged like it was no big deal and I had to fight back the need to scream at him. I knew how much a bottle of well-aged whisky could cost, and because of my grandfather's tastes for perfection in his liquor, I had an idea how much a bottle that old of what was perhaps the best whisky on the planet would cost. A bottle of the 1946 had been sold at auction a few years ago and had brought in a hefty four hundred and sixty thousand dollars. All the money had been donated to charity.

I was pretty sure that Petrova wasn't going to be at all pleased when he found his bottle of 1945 open, whoever the hell Petrova was.

Axton's grim smile turned warmer and he actually chuckled. "Of course I did. They were out for anyone to taste."

"Oh, my God," I groaned.

"Relax, Brie." Axton laughed. "I'm just kidding you. Petrova poured this himself. He's got another bottle in his safe somewhere."

I was ready to throw my glass at my ex's head, but realizing how rare and expensive the liquid was, I decided to savor the whisky first.

Still grinning, Axton glanced around the room that was almost overflowing with musicians from every genre. "Where's Liam?"

"No clue," I told him honestly. "Figured he was off catching up with a few other rockers."

Axton lifted a brow and his face tightened, but he didn't say anything else about it. For a long while he stood there beside me, keeping me company in an odd sort of way. I was actually kind of glad to have him there. It made me feel a little more like I belonged at the party. I wished it had been Liam standing there with me, though.

After a while, someone called out to Ax and he excused himself to go speak to the guy who obviously looked like he wanted to talk to him. Left alone, I took the last small sip of my Macallan and decided it was time to find Liam and head home.

The house was even bigger than I'd first assumed, something that was made blaringly obvious to me as I searched both the first and the second floor for Liam. I'd already sent two texts asking where he was and if we could go home yet, but hadn't gotten a return message.

I was about to give up when I heard Liam's distinctive laugh coming from behind one of the bedroom doors at the end of the east wing of the gigantic house. I stopped outside the door and pressed my ear against it.

My heart clenched when I heard a female giggle. Clenching my hands at my sides, I was ready to barge in and start scratching eyes out when I heard another laugh that caused me to pause. I was sure I knew the laugh, but couldn't place it.

Confused, I eased the door open and peeked my head around. Liam was sitting on a chair across from a king-sized bed. Across from him was a girl I didn't immediately recognize, with dark hair pulled back into an elegant twist and diamonds dripping from her ears and neck. Beside her sat Cole Steel.

I opened the door a little farther and stepped into the room. "Liam?"

His head snapped up and when he saw me standing in the doorway, his face split into a grin. "Hey, Brie. Come in and say hello to Cole and…" He paused and frowned at the chick beside Cole. "What was your name again?"

Disappointment flashed in the chick's eyes but she gave him a bright smile. I narrowed my eyes on her. Who the hell was this bitch? "Sonja," she said with a slight accent that I couldn't place right away. Swedish or maybe even German were my closest guesses.

"Yeah, Sonja. She's Petrova's sister or some shit." Liam stood and I crossed to him, sending the bitch a smirk as he wrapped his arm around my waist.

That's right, skank. He's mine.

"It's good to see you, Cole," I told the old rocker, not even bothering to acknowledge the chick with a greeting. She wasn't worth my time or the energy to as much as blink at her.

Cole Steel chuckled. "You too, Gabriella. Saw you drinking some of Petrova's whisky a few minutes ago with Ax. How was it?"

I shrugged. "Probably the best whisky I've ever tasted," I told him honestly. It was still singing through my blood. "You should try a glass. If Axton hasn't drunk it all."

"I might do that."

"I'm tired, Liam," I murmured as I snuggled against his side, fighting back a yawn. "Can we go home now?"

"Of course, babe." He pressed a kiss to my temple before offering his hand to Cole. "Good seeing you, man." When he turned his blue eyes to Sonja, I instinctively moved even closer to him. I recognized the look in her eyes as hunger and wanted to grab her hair and rip out a few patches to make sure she understood that all she would ever get to do was look when it came to Liam Bryant.

He was mine.

"Nice to meet you, Sonja." Liam gave her a small smile before grasping my hand and linking our fingers together.

It didn't take long before we were in the back of the limo heading toward West Hollywood. I curled up against Liam and closed my eyes. All in all, the night hadn't been bad. I'd received a Grammy and gotten to go home with the man who owned my heart.

Yeah, that made it just about perfect.

Chapter Fourteen

Gabriella

TWO YEARS AGO

Jordan's giggles could be heard from somewhere in my bedroom. I grinned to myself as I took my time searching for him. He loved to hide in my closet and I always let him think he had me fooled for a good five minutes before giving up and pretending to cry because I couldn't find him. Jordan loved it, ate it up like cake, and always gave me big, wet kisses to console me because I couldn't find him.

My favorite little man had spent last night with me, and his mother was going to pick him up in less than an hour, which gave us just enough time to have a fun game of hide-and-seek. My time with Jordan was precious to me and I wouldn't give it up for anything in the world.

It had only been him and me last night, since Liam was in Malibu for some kind of male-bonding thing before Shane Stevenson's wedding. I was glad he'd gone with the rest of his band-brothers—mostly because I needed eyewitness proof that the biggest manwhore in rock history was actually getting married—but I'd missed him.

In the two years that we had been dating, we had spent very few nights apart, mostly when he was on tour. Since OtherWorld had ditched Rich Branson and signed on with Emmie as their new manager, I steered clear of his tours. Other than Liam's band-brothers, very few people knew about our relationship. I liked it that way. The media left us alone.

"Aunt Gabs!"

I paused in my pretend search for Jordan as he came running out of my bedroom with his hands closed into fists. He shook them up at me, an excited expression on his handsome little face. I could see the beautiful meshing of his mother and father in every aspect of him and knew that one day he would be a heart-breaker.

He already was, because he sure as hell broke my heart every time he smiled so sweetly up at me like he was doing right then.

Crouching down in front of him, I hugged him tight. "I thought we were playing hide-and-seek, *bambino?*"

His shook his head. "No, Aunt Gabs. I'm bored." He scrunched up his adorable face at me before waving his fists at me again. "Look what I found," he said excitedly. "Can I have it? Can I? I like candy."

I grinned. "Really? I never would have guessed." Laughing, I opened his hands to see what he'd found. If he'd been in my closet, he might have found the few pieces of caramel that I'd left in one of my jacket pockets.

Jordan opened his hand and my heart actually stopped.

No. No. No.

NO!

Cold fear washed over me like a tsunami and my stomach heaved as I stared down at the 'candy' in Jordan's hands.

Those were definitely not caramels. I had no idea what they were, but knew instantly that they weren't candy of any kind. Nausea roiled in my stomach and I forced a smile to my face so as not to freak my little man out as I took them from him. "You don't want those, *bambino*. Those are old and taste like dirt."

Disappointment darkened his eyes. "But I want a snack, Aunt Gabs."

My heart was breaking, but somehow I was able to smile for Jordan as I distracted him from the 'candy' by making him his favorite peanut butter, marshmallow fluff, banana, and honey sandwich. By the time Alexis showed up, her son was one big sticky mess and I rushed to clean him up before my beloved cousin could suspect that I wasn't in a good place.

"Is your tummy full, Jordan?" Alexis asked her son as she poured herself a cup of coffee.

"Yes, *Mamma*." He climbed down from his chair at my kitchen island and hugged his mother like he hadn't just seen her the night before. "I missed you, *Mamma*."

Alexis's face softened and she crouched down to accept a wet kiss from her son. "I missed you more," she told him softly. "I bet *Papa* missed you too. Go get your things so we can go home to him, okay?"

"Yes, ma'am."

She straightened and turned to face me with a warm smile on her beautiful face. "Was he good for you?"

I tried to make my smile genuine, but inside my mind was a mess. My hands were still shaking and I thrust them into my jeans pockets so she wouldn't see. "Always," I assured her. "Thanks for letting me have him, Lee-Lee."

"He loves you as much as I do, Gabs. You know you can see him any time you want." She took another sip of her coffee before setting the cup down on the island. Her smile dimmed as she seemed to watch me closer. Fuck, I knew I couldn't hide from her. "What's wrong?"

"Nothing," I lied. Everything. Everything was wrong. But I couldn't tell her that. If she knew what Liam had done, Jared Moreitti would kill him. I couldn't let that happen.

Alexis made a noise, letting me know that she didn't believe me and I forced a laugh. "Honest. It's nothing. I'm just a little sad that Jordan is going home and I won't get to see him for a few weeks?"

"Oh," Alexis's eyes widened. "So you're going to visit *Nonno* after all?"

I shrugged. It was as good an excuse as any. Our grandfather had been making noises that he was lonely in Connecticut. Maybe I should go visit him, get away and clear my head. But first I had to clean up the mess Liam had made. "Yeah, so I won't be able to get Jordan next weekend. Maybe not the following weekend, either."

Were there drugs in my New York apartment too? I'd have to stop over and search. Alexis didn't go to New York often, but sometimes Jared had to fly over for business and when we were all in town at the same time, I tended to keep to my weekend schedule with Jordan.

Nausea roiled in my stomach just thinking about what could be hidden in that apartment.

Ten minutes later I hugged my cousin and her son goodbye. With a tired sigh, I leaned back against the closed door and pulled the 'candy' Jordan had found from my pocket. My hands were trembling worse now as I examined the clear-wrapped pills.

What the fuck was this shit?

Pain like I'd never felt before sliced through my heart and I dropped down on the couch in my living room. What was Liam doing?

I wasn't going to make excuses for him. I'd known what he did to himself; it had never been a secret. But he'd respected me by doing that kind of thing outside of our home. I'd looked the other way when he would come home high in the past.

Six months ago he'd been forced to take mandatory rehab because of a fight he'd gotten into on his last tour. I hadn't been there, but he had been high and gotten into a fight with some drunken fan. Liam had walked away with a few bruises while the drunken fan had needed stitches.

Emmie had been able to work whatever voodoo magic she possessed and gotten him out of trouble with only the promise of showing up daily to some rehab in Beverly Hills. Since then I'd thought that he was done with drugs.

Obviously, I'd been living in a fool's paradise.

Had I been blind to the signs of Liam using again? Or had I seen them and just refused to acknowledge them? I thought we were on the road to something long-lasting, something truly special...

Slowly, the pain in my chest was replaced with something far stronger. The longer I sat there staring down at the pills in my hand, the more my blood started to boil. How dare he bring that filth into our house? He'd hidden his poison in my closet knowing that Jordan was over often. He could have found it—and had.

Flashes of what could have happened if Jordan had just eaten the 'candy' rather than asking me blinded me for a moment. Pictures of finding Jordan's lifeless body in my closet had bile rising in the back of my throat. Shuddering, I tossed the pills on the coffee table and stood. If he'd had the pills, then there was probably more.

Five minutes later I was ready to murder the man I loved. The man I thought loved me too—even if he hadn't actually said it in the two years that we'd been together. Had I blinded myself to that, too? Did he not love me, after all?

Tears burning my eyes, whether in anger or pain I wasn't sure, I picked up my phone and ran my finger over the first name that popped into my head.

I didn't like calling Axton. Liam didn't like for me to spend more time with my ex than I had to and Axton and I still tended to argue more often than anything else so I avoided him as much as possible. Our careers tossed us together, though, so it wasn't like I could avoid him forever.

Right then, however, he was the only one I knew I could trust.

It felt like the phone rang forever before he finally picked up. "This better be good," he growled.

I didn't bother to greet him. "Liam's using again, Ax. I've found three eight-balls of coke, a meth pipe…" I broke off. My hands were shaking again and I thought I might even drop the phone. "He has this shit in my apartment. Jordan is here almost every weekend. If he found this stuff—" I bit my lip to keep from crying out in pain at the very thought of losing Jordan because of Liam's habits.

Oh, God. Oh, fuck. I could have lost him. My precious little man could have put any of those things in his mouth and I would have never seen his beautiful smile again. The man I loved could have been responsible for taking away one of the most important people in my life.

I couldn't blame anyone but myself. I'd turned a blind eye because I thought my love would fix everything. Goddammit. A sob built in my throat and I fought to keep myself under control.

"I know, Brie." Axton's tone was quieter now, full of understanding. He knew how important Jordan was to me. Axton adored my little nephew, and because he had become close with Alexis during our relationship years before, Jordon even called him Uncle Ax.

I fell down on the edge of my bed and closed my eyes. "If you don't come do something with this shit, I'm going to call the cops," I threatened, not sure if I was speaking the truth or not, but I was pissed enough to do just about anything right then.

"Fuck, Brie."

"I mean it." A tear spilled free and I scrubbed the back of my free hand across my cheek angrily. "I don't care anymore. I want this junk out of my home, along with him. You can tell him that, too."

Axton blew out a frustrated breath. "Okay. Fine. I'll be there in twenty minutes. Don't touch anything. I'll help you find the rest."

"Rest? There is more of this shit?" I couldn't control the volume of my voice. *Mio Dio.* This was a fucking nightmare.

"There's always more." His tone was calm in the face of my near hysteria. "He hides that shit everywhere. Just keep calm and I'll be right over."

I was helpless to stop the tears as they fell from my eyes now. Sucking in a deep breath, I shook my head as I stared off into space, feeling lost. "I'm over this shit," I whispered brokenly. "I'm so completely over this shit."

"Twenty minutes," Axton repeated and then the phone went dead.

My phone fell to the floor beside the bed that I shared with Liam. Unable to hold back the sob that was choking me, I let it have free rein. The noise that filled my bedroom was a terrible sound, full of pain and a sadness that went soul-deep.

It was over.

I couldn't have Liam and Jordan too. Not now. Liam had made me choose the second he had decided to hide his drugs in my home. I hadn't even known it, but we had been living on borrowed time.

He had ruined everything.

"Why, Liam?" I whispered to the empty room as I wrapped my arms around my aching body. "Why?"

Chapter Fifteen

Gabriella

Nineteen Months Earlier

"I wish you would come back to California."

A sad smile lifted at my lips as I met Alexis's gaze in the phone. "Sorry, Lee-Lee. I'm not very good company right now. You would have a better night without me, trust me."

It was New Year's Eve and she was getting ready for some big party that she and Jared were throwing at their new Malibu home. I'd spent the last week with our grandfather celebrating Christmas with him, but had gone back to my New York apartment yesterday. I'd needed to be alone.

Alexis had FaceTimed me as she was getting ready and I'd been relieved to see her face, hear her sweet voice.

It had been two months since I'd last seen Liam. I hadn't spoken to him since before he'd left my West Hollywood apartment to go out with OtherWorld the night before Shane Stevenson's wedding. There had been no phone calls, no texts, not even a damn email.

Why hadn't he tried to contact me?

Why hadn't he tried to fight for me? For us?

I didn't know the answers and the not knowing was leaving me feeling lost.

Axton had told me Liam was in rehab. That he'd gone on his own this time. For the first time, Liam had walked into rehab without someone having to threaten him with something unless he got clean. He was doing it for himself this time.

Part of me hoped he was doing it for me, too.

It had taken two weeks before I'd calmed down after finding all those drugs in my apartment. Two weeks to breathe a little easier. Two weeks before I'd started doubting myself and the decision to break up with Liam without hearing his side of the story. I'd argued with myself for over a week about being so hasty in throwing Liam out of my life.

Halfway through week four, I'd gotten mad at myself for doubting my decisions. Liam had been the one to make me choose. He had brought things into my home that could have endangered the most precious person in my life. It was his fault that we weren't together any longer. He had broken us.

He had broken me.

I'd been alternating between doubting myself and hating Liam. I missed him, worried about him. Every night before I fell asleep, I wondered if he was okay, if he was getting better. I would sleep for a few hours and then wake up with tears on my face because I missed him so much.

I wanted him in bed beside me, holding my hand, kissing my fingertips until I fell back to sleep. My heart would break a little more when I would realize that that wasn't going to happen. Liam was gone. He wasn't mine anymore.

The anger would flood back in and I would have to get out of bed, distract myself from the churning emotions that were slowly driving me toward insanity. I wanted to hit him, wanted to make him hurt just as much as I was hurting...

I wanted to hold him.

"Well, if you won't come back to California, then Jordan and I will just have to come to New York. Jared's brother and sister-in-law are flying in from Rome so we were thinking of coming out anyway. You, my dear cousin, just made up my mind." Alexis grinned and it was so infectious that my own smile didn't feel quite so forced for a moment. "I miss you, Gabs."

"Miss you more, Lee-Lee," I whispered around a sudden knot of emotion clogging my throat.

The sound of Jared's voice coming from somewhere in the distance had Alexis ending the call. I blew her a kiss before tossing the phone aside and picking up the remote to unmute the television. I'd been flipping through the channels before Alexis had called.

A rerun of some crime show was on and I quickly flipped the channel when I saw decomposed bones. Yuck.

I settled on one of the New Year's Eve countdown specials and curled my legs up under me as I half watched the show. Around ten thirty I decided to make some popcorn and had just gotten up when the commercial that was on was interrupted by the local news.

"...We don't have confirmation on the other driver, but we just learned that the driver of the Ferrari is Liam Bryant. The bassist for OtherWorld has been reportedly in rehab for the past two months and has recently been released. Police haven't said if Bryant was at fault, but that the rocker is in critical condition..."

All the air seemed to leave my lungs and I dropped back down onto the edge of the couch. Liam was hurt?

In a car accident?

No. No, that couldn't be right. He couldn't be hurt. The news had gotten it wrong, surely.

With trembling hands I reached for my phone and pulled up the first social media app I came to. The first thing I saw was a picture of Liam standing beside his gray Ferrari. The picture was old, had been taken several months before our breakup. Below the picture was the same news that I'd just heard on television.

I focused on the name of the hospital that the article said Liam was at. The trembling had spread from my hands, expanding to the rest of my body. I tried to stand but my legs were so shaky I fell back onto the couch almost immediately. Biting back a sob, I texted the car service that my grandfather always had on standby for me and Alexis whenever we needed it. There was no way I was going to be able to drive when I was feeling like this, and getting a taxi on New Year's Eve would have taken a miracle anyway.

It took me fifteen minutes to get downstairs on my wobbly legs. Thankfully, the car was already there and the driver was holding my door open for me. I could barely breathe through the lump in my throat, but somehow I told the driver where I needed to go.

By the time the driver stopped in front of the hospital, there were media vans everywhere. I didn't wait for the driver to open my door. Getting out, I sprinted toward the main entrance, my only thoughts being to get inside and see Liam for myself. It had to be all a big mistake. It couldn't have been as bad as the media had made it seem.

Please, God. Please, please, please let him be okay.

A huge man in a suit moved in front of the entrance before I could reach it. I blinked up at him and then realized that he wasn't alone. He had a partner standing just a few feet to his right who was as big as he was.

"No one goes in or out at the moment, miss," the man blocking my way informed me.

"I'm here to see Liam Bryant. I'm his girlfriend."

The big man didn't even bat an eye. "I don't care if you're the president's girlfriend. You aren't getting in."

"But…"

"Leave or I will escort you off the property, miss."

Fucking Emmie. She had put these goons there. She was the reason I couldn't get in to see Liam. If she had been standing there right then, I would have scratched up her pretty face.

I didn't have time to be angry, though. I needed to get in and knew there was only one way to do that. I needed help from the one person who would bother to help and who Emmie wouldn't say no to.

It took longer than I was happy with to get to Axton's apartment. I'd been trying to call and text him the entire drive over but he wasn't answering. Stepping off the elevator on his floor, I immediately knew why. He was throwing one hell of a party. People were spilling out of the apartment when I opened the door.

Muttering a curse, I pushed my way through the crowd and found Axton sitting on his couch in the living room. "Axton," I called as I hurried toward him. "Ax!"

He didn't move as I continued to call out to him. Just sat there, staring off at nothing and no one in particular. He didn't seem to notice the people around him and I was sure that he didn't hear anything either.

Unwilling to waste another second, I drew my hand back and slapped him across his handsome face. His lashes fluttered a few times before he glared up at me. "What the fuck, Gabriella?"

A sob built in my throat and I couldn't form words. Fresh tears spilled from my eyes as they had been doing since I'd realized that Liam was in trouble. Concern filled Axton's face and he stood, grasping my arms tightly. "What is it? Jordan?"

I shook my head. "No," I choked out. "Liam… It's all over the news. He was in an accident. A drunk driver. Some are saying it's his fault. Others are saying he was completely sober." I'd been watching all my social media apps for more news. The conflicting news reports and speculations were driving me crazy. "But they all say he's in critical condition."

I grabbed both his arms, holding on tight. "No one will fucking tell me anything." I'd tried to call the hospital but no one was saying anything. "I can't get past the guard at the hospital. They won't let me near him. Please, Ax. Please, help me." I lowered my head as the tears fell faster. "Please. I need to see him. I need to talk to him," I whispered. "I never should have broken up with him."

With a vicious curse, Axton took my hand and pulled me out of the apartment.

I was blind to anything but my own misery as we made the drive back to the hospital. As I expected, the guards let Axton in without any issues. When they moved to block me, however, Axton pulled me against his side. "She's with me," he barked.

The man moved aside and Axton released me as we stepped into the elevator. A trail of guards guided us to where Liam was. The trail ended outside a waiting room and I was nearly dancing with anxiety by the time Axton opened the door.

Four people were in the large room. Drake Stevenson stood off by himself while Linc Spencer and Natalie Stevenson sat on either side of Dallas Bradshaw. She was a nurse now, I remembered. She would know what was happening.

It didn't matter that no one in that room liked me. Nothing mattered except finding out how Liam was. "How is he?" I asked the only person who could have possibly have held the answers I so desperately needed.

The beautiful blonde jumped to her feet, hate shining out of her blue eyes as she stepped closer to me. Linc wrapped his thick arms around her waist, stopping her from coming closer. "You would fucking know if you hadn't turned your back on him."

I wished Linc would release her. Having Dallas beat the hell out of me would have hurt a hell of a lot less than the pain I was feeling thinking of Liam hurting—that I might lose him forever.

A sob bubbled up in my chest and ripped itself free. "I know," I whispered.

I never should have ended things with Liam. Never. I should have made him go to rehab when we first got together. I had been such a coward, too scared of losing him and turning a blind eye to his drug problem. This was my fault.

It was entirely my fault that I might lose him forever.

No. I can't lose him. Please, God. Please.

I'd been sitting in the waiting room for what felt like forever. No one spoke to me except for the few times Alexis had been able to sit with me. It didn't matter to me. Wasn't like I would have spoken to them if they had. I was too destroyed. If Liam didn't wake up soon, I was going to lose what little was left of my sanity.

Now, after a week in the hospital, Liam was finally waking up. As soon as he'd started showing signs of wakefulness, his nurse had come and gotten Dallas. I hadn't asked if I could go too, just followed right on her heels. I needed to see him, needed to know he was going to be okay.

My heart was racing as I entered the ICU room. A nurse was already checking Liam's vitals and Dallas was standing at the foot of the bed alternating between frowning down at him and then up at the monitors. I didn't know what she was seeing but after a few seconds her face cleared and she smiled down at a drowsy-eyed Liam.

Seeing him lying in that damn hospital bed never failed to make my chest hurt, but now, seeing his eyes open, some of the pain around my heart eased. He was really awake.

Oh, thank God. Thank God!

Tears of relief blinded me as I moved forward. "Liam," I whispered. "Oh God, I'm so happy to see you."

His whole face changed when he turned those blue eyes on me. A parade of emotions flashed through his eyes. There was relief just as strong as my own, quickly followed by hope, then pain and regret. All of that faded in the blink of an eye, though, as he clenched his jaw and glared up at me.

"What the fuck are you doing here?" he growled.

I stopped mid-step, less than a few feet away from his bedside. The pure venom in his voice chilled me to the bone. "Liam…"

"No." His voice rose. "I don't want to hear it. You don't belong here. I don't want you here." Pain sliced through me like a white-hot blade. I couldn't breathe for the pain. "We're over. Remember?"

Fresh tears flooded my eyes, making it almost impossible to see his face. I sucked in a deep breath, knowing if I didn't speak now I might never get another chance to say it. "I know and I'm sorry. I never should have ended things with us. I realize now that you are worth fighting for. Please, don't be like this. I love you. Let me stay." I was begging, but I didn't care.

I felt like my very life was at stake in that moment. If Liam kicked me out, if he wouldn't let me fix what I'd done, then I would be lost.

Through my tears, I saw him turn his head away, his gaze locking with Dallas's. "Get her the fuck out of here!" he raged. "The sight of her is turning my stomach. Make her go away, D. Now."

Everything inside of me went numb. Even my tears stopped, as if my body had completely shut down. He really did want me gone. I made him sick. Oh fuck, I couldn't breathe.

I was losing him.

He hated me.

Gabriella

No. I can't lose him. Please...

The feel of a calloused thumb rubbing circles on my palm pulled me out of my nightmare. I sighed in relief and tried to shift my hand closer to that soothing contact. When my hand actually obeyed, I tried to open my eyes, seeing how much of my brain was actually functioning.

My lashes lifted slightly and I tried harder. The dim lighting of an overhead light fixture greeted my eyes and I blinked a few times before I could focus on any one thing. All I could make out were shadows, and none of them made any sense to my pain-fogged mind. Groaning, I shifted my head, searching for the source of the still caressing thumb.

"Brie?" A hoarse voice greeted my ears and I tried to focus on the man who was sitting beside my bed. The soothing circles stopped and a warm hand tightened around my fingers. "Keep your eyes open, Brie. Please, baby, please. I need to see them."

Hope was stronger than the pain that was searing through me and I tried to obey, but my eyes wouldn't stay open for more than a second or two at a time. I wasn't scared, though. I knew who was there now. Liam. Everything inside of me breathed a sigh of relief and I found the energy to actually smile. "You...you're here," I murmured, unable to get my voice louder than a whisper. "Liam."

He was there. He was okay. Thank you, God. Thank you.

"Yes, baby. I'm right here and I'm not going anywhere."

Was that a sob I heard in his voice? No, it couldn't have been. Liam never cried. Deciding that I was imagining things, I tried to keep my eyes open for longer but didn't succeed. I started to drift back to sleep unwillingly. So tired, so much pain...

Reality shot through me as I realized why I was in so much pain and somehow my eyes snapped open. I focused on the man sitting beside my bed, his blue eyes bloodshot and damp. "Mia," I breathed. "Is Mia...?" I couldn't bring myself to finish. Couldn't bear the thought of that beautiful little girl being hurt. Or worse...

"She's fine," he assured me, tears running unchecked down his beautifully masculine face. "A few scrapes and scared, but she's fine. You saved her, Brie."

Relief washed through me and my eyes fluttered closed once again. "Glad she's...o-okay."

"Brie, you need to rest, but I need you to promise you aren't going to leave me." Liam's hold on my hand tightened. "Swear you're not going to give up on me."

If I could have snorted right then I would have, but I couldn't find the energy. Plus I knew that it was going to hurt like a bitch if I did. I didn't want to hurt more than I already did, but didn't he realize that I wasn't ever going to leave him? I loved him too much to ever leave him willingly. I'd tried that once and it hadn't ended well for either one of us. "I'm...not going...anywhere. Promise."

"I love you, Brie. I love you so fucking much."

My lips lifted in a smile, sure that I was dreaming again...

Liam

Tears poured unashamedly down my face as I lifted Gabriella's hand to my lips and kissed her soft palm.

I'd been sitting in her ICU room for over five hours and for the last hour of that she had moaned in her sleep as if she were in pain. The thought of her in pain had ripped me apart and I'd called for the nurse to have them give her something. It hadn't been time for her meds, however, and I thought I was going to lose my mind having to hear those pain-filled little moans. Then she had started thrashing her head back and forth and I'd realized she was waking up.

She had opened her eyes, promised she wasn't going to leave me, then fallen back to sleep. My girl was going to be okay, I could feel it.

Now that I knew she was going to be okay, there was so much I needed to do. I wasn't going to let her go again. There was no way in hell I was going to go on living without her. I would fight for her, beg her if I needed to, but I wasn't going to back down.

Behind me the door opened and the doctor and his nurse walked in. "So, she's awake."

I nodded, knowing they must have been watching from the nurses' station just outside the door. I was thankful they had given me a few minutes alone with her and hadn't rushed in to start poking and prodding her immediately. But I could tell from the look on Dr. Schiller's face that he was going to kick me out so he could do just that now.

The thought of her in more pain made my gut churn. Standing, I leaned over and brushed a kiss over Gabriella's forehead before turning to face the doctor. "Make sure she gets something for the pain. I don't want her hurting."

Schiller nodded, smiling understandingly. "We'll make sure she gets comfortable. Go let your family know she's awake. I'm sure her cousin wants to know, and I heard that her aunt has arrived."

My jaw clenched. So Carina Moreitti had finally made it. It had only taken three damn days. The woman was a slave to her business and didn't let anything pull her away from work unless it was a major emergency. I figured her niece getting shot and nearly dying would have been considered one, but obviously I'd been wrong. Alexis had told me that her mother was in the middle of negotiations with some big-time designer and couldn't leave Milan until they were over.

I'd only met the woman a handful of times and each occasion had left me with a bitter taste in my mouth. The woman who had basically raised Gabriella hated me, and the feeling was mutual. Although I had to admit that I would rather face Carina than her father any day of the week.

I hadn't thought of the old man not being at the hospital with the rest of Gabriella's family until the day before. Alexis had dropped a huge bomb on me when she told me that the old man had suffered a heart attack and had died recently. I knew how much Gabriella had loved that old fucker, and it was only because of her that I was sorry he was gone. If not for my girl, I might have spit on his grave.

Reaching the waiting room, I paused outside the door and raked my hands over my face. Fuck, I was tired. With Dallas's help I was able to manage my pain and with all my friends and family behind me, the cravings were easy to handle. Now that Gabriella was awake I knew I would be okay. That didn't mean I wanted to go in that room and face Carina Moreitti, though.

"Everything okay, Mr. Bryant?"

I lifted my head to look at the guard who had just spoken to me. I wasn't sure what shifts Seller's men were working on but I remembered the man in front of me well. I saw him about as often as I saw the roadies who worked for us. This big man had rarely spoken to me and I'd rarely paid him any attention, but having him speak to me now calmed some of the chaos storming through me.

I gave him a grim smile. "It's getting better, dude. She's awake."

Nothing in the man's face changed but I thought I saw something like relief flash in his eyes. "Good to hear."

With a nod, I opened the door and stepped inside. The room wasn't quite as full as it had been the last time I'd been in there. Jared Moreitti was gone and Emmie and the other Demons were still absent. Several voices halted when I entered the waiting room and I shifted my gaze to the loudest mouth in the small group that I knew had been talking about me.

"Why are they letting you back there with her?" Carina demanded, fire blazing in her eyes. "You aren't family and you sure as hell aren't anything to her."

I didn't bother to answer her as I turned my eyes to Alexis. "She's awake," I told her and her shoulders seemed to fall under the weight of her relief. "The doctor is in with her now and is going to make her comfortable. Maybe you should come back with me next time."

Alexis's smile was brighter than I'd seen it in a long time. "I will. Thank you, Liam. You've been so strong through all of this and that's helped me keep my sanity. I really appreciate everything you've done."

"What the hell has he done?" Carina demanded and I clenched my jaw, refusing to fall to her level. Whatever she had to say, she could say. It was probably the truth anyway. "Nothing but hurt her, that's what. She wouldn't have even been at that damn festival if it weren't for him. He's gotten her addicted to him, that's all this is. If it weren't for him, Gabriella wouldn't be in there…"

"Mom!" Alexis turned on her mother with a look in her dark eyes that I'd never seen before. "You know nothing about it. Nothing. Gabs loves Liam, and that is something you will never understand because you've only ever been in love with your job. So back off. He's been here every day, every damn hour. Yet you are just now getting here. That shows me exactly who cares for her more and right now you are falling dangerously low on the list of people I want near her."

Carina's eyes widened. "Alexis, what—"

"No, Mom." Alexis shook her head, forcefully cutting off her mother. "You don't get to come in here three days too late and start spewing hate about a man who has been in agony over the possibility of losing Gabs. So you either shut your damn mouth or I'll have one of those scary men in suits outside escort you back to your hotel."

The older Moreitti female clamped her mouth shut and moved away from her daughter. The fire had left her eyes as she dropped down onto a chair close to one of the windows. Alexis gave me an apologetic smile before moving to the opposite side of the room, as far away from Carina as the room permitted.

I was blown over. Alexis had taken up for me. That was… Yeah, that was a little crazy.

I felt a soft hand touching my arm and looked down to find Marissa beside me. She and Wroth had moved to stand with me, offering me support in the face of Carina's wrath. I wrapped my arms around my sister's shoulders and let her strength—her goodness—soak into me.

I'd been okay with Carina bad-mouthing me; I could have taken it. Things like that rolled off my back. Yet, having Alexis take up for me like she had was affecting me. Very few people had ever done that for me. That, on top of all the other shit I'd had to deal with over the last three days, was making it hard for me to keep myself in check.

I hugged my sister for a long time, needing her love more than I needed anything else right then. Eventually the tightness in my chest and the stinging in my eyes started to ease and I pulled back enough to press a kiss to Marissa's cheek. Kind blue eyes gazed lovingly up at me. "So, she's awake?"

My lips eased into a small smile. "Yeah, Riss. She's awake. I talked to her for a minute or two before she fell back to sleep. She's going to be okay, I can feel it."

Tears filled my sister's eyes. "That's great, Li. I'm so glad."

I stepped back and she moved to wrap her arms around Wroth's waist. She looked as tired as I felt but I selfishly wanted to keep her close. "Thanks for being here, Rissa."

"There's no other place we would be, Li." She looked up at her husband. "Right?"

"Yeah, bro. We're here as long as you need us." Wroth's deep, almost animalistic voice was low.

I clenched my jaw to keep from doing something stupid—like crying like a pussy over the love I saw shining out of my cousin's eyes. Sure, I'd done enough crying the last few days to fill a fucking ocean, but this was different. All my life all I'd ever wanted was to be like Wroth, but I'd fucked that up from the get-go. I'd taken the wrong paths in life, and then had taken the long way back to a place where I could even begin to feel worthy of my family's love.

A hard hand fell on my shoulder, giving it an almost painful squeeze, telling me that Wroth knew what I was feeling and that he loved me. I lowered my head and sucked in a deep breath before stepping back. "Yeah, okay. Thanks."

"Liam?"

I lifted my head to find Annabelle just a few feet away. "Does the doctor have any news? Emmie wants Natalie and I to do another press conference updating everyone on her progress in about two hours."

"He should be out to speak with us soon, Anna-Banana." I shifted my gaze from her to the shorthaired chick standing with a phone in her hand, Devlin Cutter right beside her. "Nat?" I called out to her and her head immediately snapped up. "Can I talk to you?"

She moved forward and Devlin started to follow. "No," I told him and he stopped. "I need to talk to her alone."

My friend shrugged and leaned back against the wall where he'd been the majority of the time he was in the waiting room. Natalie pocketed her phone as she drew closer and I took her hand, pulling her out of the room. Outside, I pulled her down the corridor to a spot that looked discreet enough before stopping and facing her.

"What's up?" she asked, her blue-gray eyes full of concern. "Is she really going to be okay?"

I nodded. "Yeah, I think she is." I thrust my hands into the pockets of my jeans and leaned against the wall. Now that I had her out here, I didn't know how to ask for what I needed. Muttering a curse, I jumped right into it. "You're as good as Emmie...right?"

Her eyes widened. "I like to think I am, but no. I'm not even in Emmie's hemisphere yet. Why? What do you need?"

I swallowed hard, nervous as hell. Why, I couldn't have said. I knew what I wanted, knew what I had to do—or at least hoped that I knew—to get Gabriella back. So what was my problem?

Maybe because I knew how much was riding on it...

Chapter Seventeen

Gabriella

I heard someone moving around and once again I tried to open my eyes. If it was the doctor or his evil nurse coming back to poke and prod my aching body again, I was going to seriously slap a bitch. They had spent forever moving me every which way and touching parts of my body that were still screaming in agony.

Both had left with the promise of pain relief. I wasn't sure how long ago that had been or even if someone had already brought me the medication. All I knew was that I was in some serious pain and all I wanted was to see Liam again.

Had he really been there or had that been a dream? I was almost scared to ask. If he hadn't really been there, then that meant he hadn't actually said he loved me... And I wasn't sure if I could handle knowing that just yet.

"Who's there?" I called out when I couldn't get my eyes to fully cooperate. I was so tired, in so much pain, that I could barely lift my lids.

"You're awake!"

Everything inside of me went still and then I breathed a sigh of relief as I lifted my hand. "Lee-Lee."

Her fingers were trembling when she wrapped them around my hand. "Oh, God, Gabs. You scared me so bad." I heard a sob in her voice and felt my eyes sting with tears. "You can't do things like that to me. If something happened to you, I don't know what I would do."

"Sorry," I whispered and tried to keep my eyes open so that I could see her beloved face. "I had to do...something. Mia..." I broke off and closed my eyes tight, fighting back flashes of what had happened leading up to being shot. "Liam said she's okay... Or was that a dream?"

"It wasn't a dream, baby."

A small gasp escaped me at the sound of his voice. I hadn't realized that there was more than one person in my room. So it hadn't been a dream. Liam had been there, and he'd said he loved me. I swallowed hard and kept my eyes closed, feeling suddenly shy. It was a new feeling to have, especially around this man.

I heard footsteps approaching and found the energy to tighten my hold on Alexis's hand. Moments later I felt my hospital bed shifting near my head before his lips brushed over my closed eyes. "How are you feeling, baby?" he asked in a quiet voice. "Are you in pain?"

"A l-little," I murmured.

"I'll speak to the doctor," he promised and I felt him moving away.

Part of me wanted to stop him, but another, bigger, part wanted a few minutes to gather myself. I wasn't used to feeling like this. Vulnerable, shy, weak. Was it because I was so helpless right then, needing help from everyone around me because I was as weak as a newborn? Or was it just Liam who was making me feel like this? I didn't know and I hated feeling like that.

"Hold on just a second, Gabs. Let me pull a chair closer so I can sit with you." Alexis released my hand and then I heard the sound of a chair's legs scraping on the floor seconds before she grasped my hand once more. At her soothing touch, I let out a relieved sigh and turned my head toward her.

"How long have you been here?"

Alexis rubbed her soft hands over the back of my knuckles. "I got here the morning after the shooting. I've been here for three days. Mom's here, but I don't think you should see her just yet. She's running her mouth and we've been arguing."

I grimaced. "What did she say to him?" I knew she had to have said something to Liam.

The few times I'd brought Liam around her, she'd seemed to take pleasure in annihilating him. She hadn't been able to find one good thing about him. He had too many tattoos. His hair was always messy. His clothes were never good enough. He drove the wrong kind of car. I was sure that if Liam had been anyone other than a rocker, my aunt wouldn't have batted an eye at the man I'd told her I was in love with. She'd been the same way when I'd been with Axton, but even then it hadn't been nearly as extreme as the way she was around Liam.

"We can talk about that later. Just know that she's in the waiting room and I'm not letting her through the ICU ward doors anytime soon. You don't need to be upset."

I nodded. "Okay. Is Jared with you? Jordan?" Christ, I really wanted to see my precious little man right then, but I didn't want to scare him. I probably looked hideous and I didn't want to give him nightmares about seeing his Aunt Gabs like this.

"Jared got here not long after I did. We had to take different flights because there weren't enough seats and it was impossible to charter anything the other night. Vince brought up Jordan. They are all at the hotel right now. Jordan has been impatient and cranky so I had Jared take him for a good sleep and something to eat. He's been playing in the pool at the hotel, so he's content for the moment."

"Good." Some of the tension in my chest eased and I blinked over at Alexis, finally able to keep my eyes open for longer than a few seconds.

When I finally got a good look at my beloved cousin, fresh tears burned my eyes. "Oh, Lee-Lee." Her hair needed brushing and her beautiful face was pale with dark circles underneath her eyes, which were bloodshot from lack of sleep and crying. "I'm sorry."

"Don't be sorry, Gabs. I'm fine. And I know this wasn't your fault. It's not like you wanted to be shot. What you did? That was a really brave thing. You're a hero."

I nearly snorted. "Not quite."

Her lips lifted in a smile that calmed some of the ache in my heart. "Everyone is saying you are. The media, the feds, even Emmie."

My eyes widened at that last part. "Emmie?"

"She was here most of the last three days. She's been working with Annabelle to make sure that everything is taken care of. No one has had to do anything. The Feds are up-to-speed on your condition and the media has been getting regular reports. The only time I saw her leave was hours ago when her husband showed up and asked her to return to their bus. Mia needs her mother."

I shook my head in disbelief. I didn't know what to make of that, but I didn't want to examine it too closely. Not yet.

The door to my room slid open and Liam entered with a nurse right behind him. My eyes found him and stayed, unable to look away from the best sight I'd seen in forever. He looked tired and he was limping, making me wonder how much pain he was in right then. I bit the inside of my cheek as I took the rest of him in.

He was just as pale as Alexis and his eyes were glassy, bloodshot. "Are you okay?"

His lips lifted into a tired half smile. "I think that's my line, baby. Now that you're awake, I'm perfect."

The nurse moved around to the other side of my bed with a needle-less syringe in her hand filled with some kind of clear liquid. I watched as she went about cleaning off my IV line. "What is that?"

"The good stuff," the nurse told me with a grin. "You'll be feeling nothing in about sixty seconds."

"No!" I told her as she started to put the syringe into my IV line. "I don't want to be out of it yet." Fuck, I was barely awake as it was. I wanted to soak up the sight of Alexis and Liam. I wanted to ask more questions. I wanted... So many damn things.

"You're in pain, Gabs." Alexis rubbed her hand up and down my arm, trying to calm me. She was right. I was in pain, more pain than was probably humanly possible to withstand. "Let her give you the medication. We aren't going anywhere."

Two tears spilled from my eyes. "P-promise?" I whispered as I looked up at Liam. He was the one I was really asking. I was glad Alexis was there, but I *needed* Liam to stay.

Something in his eyes darkened, or maybe I was just seeing things from all the pain I was in. He leaned over the bed and brushed a kiss over my forehead. "I promise, Brie. As long as you're here, so am I." He lifted his hand and used his thumb to wipe away my tears. "It's okay, baby. Let the nurse do her job and get some rest. I'll watch over you."

The hand that the IV was in lifted and I caught his fingers. Turning my face into the pillow, I held on tight as a few more tears fell. "You'll be here when I open my eyes?"

"Baby, you're killing me with those tears," he muttered with a groan. His lips were on my cheek now, kissing away my tears. "I swear on Marissa's life that I'll be here. Okay? I'm not going anywhere, little Brie."

He took my hand and held it while the nurse put the syringe into the IV line. I didn't watch as she pushed the liquid inside, but I knew the instant she did. My arm burned from the medication, causing my arm to ache for a long moment. I kept my eyes on Liam, wanting him to be the last thing I saw before the pain meds took over and I was pulled under again.

My vision blurred and I blinked my eyes, fighting the effects of the powerful narcotic. "Liam."

He smiled down at me. "Right here, baby. I'm right here."

I didn't dream. At least, I didn't think I did, because I couldn't remember dreaming.

I woke up twice over an unknown period. The first time, Alexis and Liam were sitting beside my bed. Alexis was holding my hand and running her nails up and down my arm in the way I knew Jordan liked. Liam sat closer to the head of my bed, his hand resting beside my face and every now and then he would caress my cheek with the back of his knuckles.

I'd watched them for a while. Neither had spoken, but they seemed to be comfortable enough with the silence. Without realizing it, I'd fallen back to sleep.

The second time I'd opened my eyes, Alexis was gone but Liam was still there. He'd switched seats and was leaning forward. One of his big, rough hands was holding onto mine as he rested his head on the bed, kissing my fingertips tenderly. The lights were dim so I couldn't make out much of his face, but he looked tired.

I should have told him to go back to his bus or even a hotel. It was obvious he needed some decent sleep. Yet the thought of asking him to go—and him actually leaving—terrified me.

Noticing that I was awake, Liam lifted his head. "Okay?"

I nodded. The pain meds were still doing their job, even if they had lost some of their original effect. "Thirsty," I mumbled. My mouth felt like it was as dry as a desert, but oddly my lips didn't feel cracked like I would have thought they would have been, considering what the rest of my body had been through over the last few days. Licking my lips, I found them coated in something minty and realized that someone had been putting salve on them.

Liam got to his feet quickly and moved to the end of my bed where a rolling table had a pitcher of water and a cup waiting. He poured half a cup and opened a straw before coming back to me. His blue eyes went from me to the water and then back, a frown scrunching up his face. "I'd lift the head of the bed if I knew it wouldn't hurt you. Let's play it safe." He lowered the cup and angled the straw toward my lips.

The first taste of the iced water felt like heaven on my tongue. I couldn't help but moan as I took a thirsty swallow. Liam pulled the cup away far too soon. "Easy," he murmured, wiping away a few drops that had spilled onto my chin. "You don't want to drink too quickly or it might all come back up."

My mouth and throat ached for more, but I didn't argue. I definitely didn't want to vomit at the moment. Not only was I sure that it would make me wish I was dead from the pain of it, but I didn't want Liam seeing me like that. For the next several minutes, Liam gave me one small sip after another until I'd finally had my fill.

He put the cup back on the table and sat back down in his chair. I couldn't help but notice his grimace in pain as he bent. "Your leg's bothering you."

Liam shrugged. "Dallas will be in to give me my shot in a little bit. I'm good until then."

My eyes widened. "Dallas? As in Dallas Cage?"

"Do you know another Dallas?" He smirked at me. "Yeah, baby. Dallas Cage. She's been here since you were brought in. Hasn't left. It's because of her that you made it to the hospital. The doctor told me…" His voice trailed off and a haunted look passed over his face. "He said that if she hadn't been there, hadn't been so well-trained, that you wouldn't have lasted more than a few minutes."

Seeing his pain was like having a knife cut into my heart. I couldn't bear it. The last thing I wanted was to cause this beautiful man pain. When he hurt, so did I. "I'm glad she was there and that she's been here with you. She's a really good friend to you." I bit the inside of my cheek, thinking about the blond woman.

Groggily, I wondered how shocked Liam would be if I told him that Dallas had been the one who had been keeping me updated on his continued recovery? It had surprised me, too, when I'd gotten that first email from her. She had been the one to reach out to me first, mere months after she had married Axton.

When I'd seen her email in my inbox, I'd been skeptical about opening it. I'd known that she was pregnant with her first child and I'd also known that she and Axton were happy. So I'd wondered what the blond chick had to say to me. I wasn't anything to her. It wasn't like we were going to start being BFFs or whatever.

After opening it, I was so glad I had. The email had been simple, strictly to the point. She had wanted to know if I was okay and if I still wanted to know how Liam was doing. I'd put her wanting to know if I was okay down to her pregnancy hormones working overtime and had emailed her back with a definite yes.

I had been almost to the point of desperation wanting to know how Liam was doing. I'd tried to ask several other people—roadies, mostly—but no one would tell me shit. Two days later I'd gotten my first update on Liam. He was doing well, was working out hard and staying clean. She hadn't gone into any personal details, like if he was seeing anyone—or, more to the point, sleeping with anyone. For that, I had been thankful.

After that I'd gotten a regular email monthly, sometimes twice a month if she was feeling particularly good-humored. We never shared details about our own lives, but I'd felt as if we had been able to at least put my past with her husband behind us.

Looking at Liam now, I decided that it wasn't the best time to tell him I'd been basically stalking him via one of his friends. Not exactly what he needed to hear right then and I wasn't sure I was strong enough to deal with it if he did get upset. So I kept my mouth closed.

The meds were still holding strong and it didn't take long before I was drifting off to sleep again.

Liam

Two days passed before the doctor thought Gabriella was showing enough of an improvement that she could be moved out of ICU. They put her in a large, private room and pulled a reclining chair up beside the bed. I wasn't sure who had told them to get the chair, but I was thankful for it. I hadn't left Gabriella's side except to use the bathroom, eat, and when the doctor kicked me out to do whatever it was he did to my girl when I wasn't around.

My leg was hurting again. I hadn't worked out in over five days and my muscles were protesting it, especially the ones in my leg. Dallas was coming in to give me a shot every few hours, but otherwise she was back at her bus with her family. Our tour was over, the last few stops on it having been canceled by Emmie, and no one was moving on until I was ready. I was thankful for that, too. Having them all, not just my band-brothers but Demon's Wings as well, to stand behind me at the moment meant a lot to me.

Gabriella was getting stronger with each passing day. She slept more often than not, but that was because of all the pain meds they were giving her. When she was awake, we didn't talk much. I preferred it that way because I didn't want to get into anything heavy until she was out of the hospital. Plus, talking seemed to cause her more pain and lowered her O2 levels even with the oxygen tubes in her nose. So, I kept quiet beside her bed and just played with her fingers, making her smile even in her sleep.

Today was day two in her private room and I knew that our reprieve from the outside world was going to be over very soon. Annabelle had told me the night before that the cops and Feds wanted to talk to Gabriella. I didn't want to put her through reliving the shooting but knew I was powerless to stop it. She would have to talk to them so that they could continue with their investigation.

Also on the list of things that I didn't want to have to put my girl through, but knew I couldn't prevent, was getting her out of bed. Doctor Schiller wanted her up and moving around, getting the soreness out and building up her lungs. I was going to be a nervous wreck. I couldn't stand it when she was in pain. The day before, she had sneezed and the whimper that had left her had nearly made me climb the fucking wall. It killed me. When she hurt, I hurt right along with her.

The nurse had come in and helped Gabriella from the bed to the bathroom to help her wash and do whatever womanly things she needed to do in there. I'd sat in the chair, my head in my hands, practically pulling out my hair as her pain-filled cries stabbed into me. I'd been ready to rip someone apart just listening. After it was over, the same nurse helped her sit in the recliner that had been my bed the night before.

She sat there with her feet propped up, a light blanket over her legs and the remote in her hand.

"They have Dish, but none of the good channels," she grumbled and tossed the remote toward me.

I caught it at the last second. "What do you want to watch?"

She rolled her eyes at me, letting me know that she was starting to feel a little better. "You think Rissa would be willing to loan me her copy of *The Wizard of Oz*?"

I grinned for what felt like the first time in years. "I can get you your own copy if you want to watch it so badly."

"I don't want you to leave," she said in a rush. "Never mind."

"I'm not going anywhere. I've told you that already." I lifted the remote and flipped the channels, leaving it when it landed on the local news station. There wasn't anything mentioned about Gabriella, the shooting, or the attempted kidnapping, but I knew that it was only a matter of time before the anchorman brought it up. "I can make a call, little Brie. I've got Natalie and Emmie on speed dial and Anna-Banana gave me her number, too."

Dark, Italian eyes narrowed on me. "Anna-Banana?"

My lips twitched at the fire in her brown eyes. *Jealous much, baby?* I didn't say anything, though. I wasn't about to add fuel to that fire. My little goddess had always been a little firecracker and I wasn't about to set her off. "I've always called her that. Did she tell you?"

Those eyes narrowed even more. "Tell me what?"

"That we grew up together. She used to live in the house between Zander and Devlin. Her brother, Noah?" She nodded and I went on. "He was our original lead singer and then one day he just up and said he was getting married and wanted to focus on a solo country career. A few weeks later, we signed with Rich Branson and were on a bus for California."

"That's crazy," she exclaimed. "What the hell was Noah thinking? I mean, Annabelle said he did pretty well for himself in the country business, but it's nothing compared to what OtherWorld has done. Why would he just leave you guys like that?"

I shrugged. "I've always wondered about that, too, but I have no idea. He just said it was something he had to do. Axton came on board a few days later, and I'm glad he did. I don't think we would have made it to where we are now without that fucker." I leaned forward in my chair and reached for her hands. "So, what do you feel like watching? I'll call someone and they will bring you whatever you want."

She linked her fingers with mine, a smile on her face that was almost shy. That both bothered me and squeezed at my heart. My girl had never been shy around me. Even before we'd gotten together she'd always been a ball-buster, not a shy little mouse. "Will you watch *August Rush* with me?"

I bit back my groan and grinned. Should have known it. Of course she would want to watch her favorite movie. How many times had we lain in bed watching that damn movie?

Something tightened in my chest. Not nearly enough times, that's how many. Lifting her fingers, I kissed each tip. "You got it, baby. Anything else?"

Gabriella shook her head. "Not that I can think of. Surprise me."

I pulled my phone from my front pocket and sent a quick text to Natalie, telling her everything I wanted. It went unanswered. Frowning, I pulled up Emmie's name and sent her the same text, getting an instant message.

Be right there.

Pocketing the phone, I sat back in my chair and watched my girl. Her eyes were half closed, her face pale, and it was obvious to me that she was exhausted. I wanted to punch her doctor in the face for making her get out of bed. She needed her rest, not to sit up like this.

We sat there in silence for the next twenty minutes. A nurse brought in her lunch and I moved out of the way so she could sort Gabriella. The rolling table was pulled up and lowered to her lap. The food looked better today than it had the day before. There was some chicken soup with crackers, Jell-O, tea that looked weak and some apple juice.

After the nurse was gone, I retook my seat and watched as Gabriella grimaced every time she lifted her arm to feed herself. By the third time she was biting back more painful whimpers and started to push the tray away.

I scooted my chair closer to her and grabbed her spoon. "Let me."

Her lashes lowered so I couldn't see her eyes and I knew that she was trying to hide her emotions from me. It's what she'd always done when she was feeling too much of something. Lifting her bowl of soup, I scooped up some of the broth and brought it to her lips.

A small smile teased at her lips before she opened her mouth and accepted the bite. "Good girl." I smirked, making her glare at me. I gave her a wink and continued to feed her the soup.

The bowl was barely half-empty before she started protesting, saying she was full. I set it down and opened the packet of crackers.

"Please?" I pouted at her when she started to protest again and she snatched two crackers from my fingers, munching on them.

Laughing, I moved the tray aside and offered her the apple juice. It was her turn to pout and I knew exactly why. "Sorry, little Brie. The doctor isn't going to let me bring you in a bottle of wine. Just close your eyes and pretend it's a good Italian blend."

"When can I get out of here?" she mumbled.

"Don't know, don't really care. Your little ass is staying as long as the doctor wants you to." She flipped me off and I couldn't help but laugh again.

Fuck, this felt good. Not the part where she was hurt—I hated that. No, I loved that I was there with her. That I got to tease her and be with her. I'd missed this. How could I have forgotten how much I loved just sitting beside her?

"You're a smartass, you know that?"

"Yeah," I assured her, smirking once more. "You've told me that plenty of times."

"And yet I still dated you for over two years... Hmm. Must have been something wrong with my head back then." She had her lashes lowered again and a teasing smile on her beautiful face.

I knew she was only teasing, but her words cut me to the quick. I'd always wondered why she had put up with me for as long as she had. I'd put this girl—my girl—through so fucking much. Any other chick would have tossed my ass to the curb from the very beginning, but not her. Not my Gabriella. She'd overlooked my flaws, had loved me despite them.

And my dumb ass had let her go.

I clenched my jaw, thinking of all the time I'd wasted with her. Where would we have been right then if I hadn't listened to her grandfather? Would we have been married by now? Have kids? Would she have been sitting on my bus with her belly softly rounded with my child growing inside of her instead of sitting in that hospital recliner, hurting?

Guilt and a sense of loss burned in my chest and I sucked in a deep breath, trying to ease some of the pain. Standing, I moved to the window and glared out at the sunny afternoon sky.

"Hey," Gabriella said, sounding regretful, and I slowly turned to look at her. "I'm sorry. I didn't mean that how it sounded."

My smile was forced this time as I tried to reassure her. "I know, baby. I was just thinking…" I shook my head. "It doesn't matter. Are you comfortable? Are you hurting?"

"I'm fine for now. Come sit with me again. Please?" She held out her hand and I took it without hesitation. "I really am sorry."

"You have nothing to be sorry about, little Brie." I kissed the back of her hand and linked our fingers. "I don't know how you put up with me, baby. I'm just thankful that I had as long as I did with you."

Pain flashed across her face. "Liam—"

"Knock, knock."

We both looked up as the door opened and the redhead stepped inside. Gabriella tensed beside me and I rubbed my thumb over her palm to soothe her as I frowned up at Emmie. I hadn't really expected her to come herself. I figured she would have sent Natalie or any one of her other minions.

The look on her face was startling, however. Her eyes were full of something I couldn't decipher, those big green eyes clouded with a multitude of emotions. The feelings that stuck out the most were regret… and gratefulness.

In her arms was a box that I assumed was the Blu-ray player and the movies I'd asked for. The smile on her face was something I'd never seen before, full of nervousness. I stood and took the box from Emmie's arms and placed it on the bed.

She gave me a grim smile. "The last time I did you a favor, I ended up pretending to make out with you outside some nasty bathroom."

"I figured you would have sent Nat," I admitted, ignoring her comment about the bathroom incident. Now wasn't the time to admit that I'd talked Emmie into pretending to make out with me so I could push Gabriella away.

"Yeah, well, that option wasn't open for me. Natalie and Devlin ran off to Vegas to get married." My eyes nearly popped out of my head at her announcement and she laughed. "Surprised the fuck out of me too, but they had their reasons. I'm happy for them."

I nodded. "Yeah, me too." Devlin and Natalie deserved to be happy. That was all that mattered.

"So…" Emmie was back to looking nervous again. "Do you need anyone to help you set that up? I was told that it's pretty straight forward, but if you need help I can find someone?"

"No, Em. I think I can manage it."

She nodded and clasped her hands together in front of her, glancing from me to Gabriella and then back to me. After a long pause, she blew out a long sigh and glared at me. "Can you give us a minute?"

I blinked, sure that I'd heard her wrong. "What?" There was no way she wanted to be alone with Gabriella… Right?

"I need to speak to Gabriella…Brie…Gabriella, alone. It won't take long, and I promise not to upset her." She clenched her jaw and lowered her eyes to her hands. "Please, Liam."

I glanced down at Gabriella. She seemed just as shocked as I was, possibly more so. Her eyes were glued to Emmie's down-bent head, as if she were trying to figure the other chick out. After a slight hesitation, she lifted those brown eyes to mine. With a small nod she told me that it was okay to leave her.

Reluctantly, I left the room, wondering how much damage I'd have to clean up when I got back.

Gabriella

Maybe I'd woken up in an alternate universe. It would explain this moment. Nothing else could.

Emmie Armstrong wanting to speak to me? Willingly?

From the way she was acting, I was pretty sure it wasn't to bitch me out, which made this whole thing even more bizarre. I wouldn't say it was a bad thing, because honestly I kind of liked seeing Emmie looking lost for words. Which was exactly how she appeared right then.

Those big, green eyes were clouded with a mixture of emotions I couldn't easily name, and her fingers trembled even though she had her hands clasped together in front of her. But even as I got a small, cheap thrill out of seeing my sworn enemy squirm, a bigger part of me felt sorry for her. I could guess why she was there, and it was probably the only reason she would have ever been in the same room with me without us clawing each other's eyes out.

That reason made my chest ache for a reason other than the fact that my chest had been cut open—twice, from what the doctor had told me—just a few days ago. The thought of something happening to Mia made me hurt. It didn't matter that her mother and I hated each other. No child should have to go through what that beautiful little girl had.

"Look…" Emmie started, then broke off when her chin started to tremble.

Ugh. I couldn't stand this. "Emmie, stop. You don't have to do this." I didn't want this. No matter how much I'd always wanted to bring her to her knees, I didn't want to do it this way. No parent should ever feel what she was feeling right then.

"No." Emmie shook her head and clenched her jaw. "No, I have to do it." She tossed her head back and sighed up at the ceiling for a long moment before turning that bold green gaze back on me. "I owe you everything I have, Gabriella. If it hadn't been for you…"—her chin trembled again— "…I don't know what would have happened to Mia. She and Jagger are my life. Without them…" Her voice broke and she muttered a curse. Clearing her throat, she continued. "You saved her. And for that I will be forever grateful. If you need anything from me, it's yours. I would gladly give my life for yours because you nearly gave your own for my child. Thank you."

I could have been petty and told her to go to hell, I didn't need her gratitude. Any decent human being would have done the same thing I had. But we were so much alike that I knew how much this was costing her. For Emmie, this was akin to groveling and I couldn't let this strong chick torture herself like that.

"You're welcome," I murmured. "But you owe me nothing. It doesn't matter. None of it matters. Don't you see that? All I care about is that Mia is okay. This thing between you and me… That never even entered into it. We both have things that we regret. At least I know I do." I wasn't going to apologize for letting her think I'd slept with Nik all those years ago. I was pretty sure that she didn't want me to rehash that particular moment in our relationship just then. "I saw that she was in trouble and reacted. Even knowing that I would have ended up like this, I still would have done it again without hesitating." I pulled my blanket around me a little tighter, chilled at all the thoughts of what could have been had I not been there to stop Mia's kidnapping. "I'm glad she's okay..." I whispered. "I was so scared that one of the bullets had gotten her too."

A small cry left Emmie and she dropped down onto the chair that Liam had been sitting in for most of the day, as if her legs could no longer support her. "When I saw her, covered in blood, at first I thought it was hers. I'd been going out of my mind until we found her, but when I saw her like that... I nearly lost it all over again." She scrubbed her hands over her face. "Then I realized it was yours, her savior's, and all the awful things I'd ever said and done to you came flooding back to me. I'm not a nice person, Gabriella. Of course you already know that, but in that moment I would gladly have taken it all back. I would have changed places with you."

"You're a good mother, Emmie," I told her. Only a good parent would feel something that strongly. There were some parents out there who wouldn't have cared what had happened to their child and that thought made me incredibly sad. "Mia's lucky to have you."

She gave a small, humorless laugh. "It doesn't feel like it sometimes, but I would do anything for my kids. That includes selling my soul to you if that's what you want."

"Oh, please. One bitchy soul is enough for me. I'll pass, thanks," I said and before I could stop myself I snorted and then moaned from the pain I'd just inflicted on myself. *Sonofabitch that hurt!*

Emmie gave me a concerned frown. "Do you need the nurse?"

I waved her away when she started to get up. "No, I'm fine. I just sometimes forget that my chest was cracked open and a doctor played Operation with my heart a few days ago." Her face filled with horror and I actually grinned. Fuck, I'd never thought the day would come when I would actually smile at my worst enemy. Surprisingly, it kind of felt good.

Not that I was ever going to admit that out loud.

"Relax. The doctor said I'm going to be okay," I assured her.

Her face cleared a little. "Good. I'm glad." She rubbed her hands down the front of her jeans-covered legs and stood. "I should go. Mia is still a little freaked out and doesn't want me too far for very long. I need to get back to her. She's been asking if she can come see you. To thank you herself."

My heart melted a little at how sweet Mia was. "Yes, I'd like that. I'm glad she wasn't hurt."

"Me too. Thanks again, Gabriella." She held out her hand and I stared at it for a moment before finally shaking it. *Whoa, I wonder how much that cost her?* It wasn't like with that handshake we were going to suddenly be BFFs or even just friends, but I could see in her green eyes that our past was just that—in the past. Maybe we could start over. Maybe not.

It was kind of sad that it had taken something so tragic to get us to this point.

She turned to go and as I watched her leave my room, I realized that now I had to find a new worst enemy.

Damn it.

A grin spread across my face and I was still smiling when Liam returned.

Chapter Nineteen

Liam

By the end of the third day of Gabriella being in her private room, I was exhausted. More so than I'd been over the last week. I was drained to the point that I had no patience left and I sat in my chair glaring out the window as the Feds and local police took their time questioning my girl.

They had gone over her side of what had happened five times already, making her elaborate on every detail. From how pale Gabriella's face was, I knew she was either hurting, or reliving what had happened and it was really getting to her. Probably both. I was ready to grab the skinny little local cop and the pot-bellied Fed and sling them out of the room, fuck the consequences.

Hearing in Gabriella's own words what had happened, realizing exactly how close Mia had come to being shot as well, knowing that whoever had done this was a psychotic bitch, was making my hands clammy. It felt like an elephant was sitting on my chest and I realized it was panic.

She was still out there.

She. Was. Still. Fucking. Out. There.

By now she probably knew that Gabriella was awake and getting better. Was she planning on coming back to finish the job? Was my girl still in danger? Could she be waiting to strike again?

Would that crazy bitch try to take Gabriella away from me again?

Oh, fuck. I couldn't breathe.

I was going insane with all the possibilities. I wouldn't let anything happen to her, I assured myself. That bitch would have to go through me to get to my girl. She was safe now. I wasn't going anywhere and it was easier to get into Fort Knox than this hospital because of Seller's men.

It was with that thought that I was able to draw in a deep breath. Frustrated, I jerked to my feet and turned to glare at the two men standing on either side of Gabriella's bed. "That's enough," I growled at them. "She's answered your questions. Can't you see she's in pain and exhausted?"

"We're aware of that, Mr. Bryant, and we apologize. But we have to know everything," the skinny local cop tried to be explain.

"And she's told you everything she remembers." I crossed the room and opened the door for them. "If you have any other questions, relay them through Annabelle Cassidy or Emmie Armstrong. She's done."

The two men pressed their lips together in a firm line but didn't argue with me. Putting away their notebooks and the little recorder the Fed had been using, they left. I watched until they had reached the elevator before turning my gaze to the two guards standing outside the door.

"No more visitors. I don't care who it is. She's going to sleep and doesn't need to be disturbed."

They both nodded but didn't speak so I closed the door and moved toward Gabriella's bed.

Her eyes were full of wary amusement as I approached. "Thanks for saving me. I was starting to feel like I'd done something wrong with the way they kept pressing me for more details."

"You look tired. Try to go to sleep. Do you need anything for pain?" I pushed a few strands of freshly washed hair away from her face.

She'd pleaded and pleaded with the staff to wash her hair all day. They had told her they could give her some dry shampoo but she threw a fit over that. She'd wanted clean hair, she'd yelled. It was hard for her to sleep with dirty hair; that's the way it had always been.

The nurses hadn't relented, however, so I'd called Annabelle who had shown up with Alexis, Marissa and two local stylists who had given Gabriella's hair a thorough washing as well as a head, shoulder, and face massage. She had been so relaxed that she had fallen asleep. During the whole thing, I'd stood at the door with Seller's guards and dared the nurses to interrupt.

Sure, I knew that they had only been doing their job and following protocol, but if my girl wanted something, I was going to make sure that she got it. What the hell could washing her hair hurt?

"I still have a little while before I need the pain meds." She lifted her hands, a sleepy look in her eyes. "Come lie with me."

I looked down at her in that narrow hospital bed. I would have given anything to be able to lie down beside her and hold her. Every fiber inside of me was screaming to do it, but I didn't want to hurt her. That bed wasn't big enough for me and her and all the tubes that were still connected to her. She still had a chest tube in to keep fluid out of her left lung. The IV was still connected, although they had to move it the day before because the vein had perforated. She continued to wear her oxygen but the doctor had reduced the flow so she wasn't getting nearly as much as she had been.

"I can't, baby. I don't want to hurt you." I stroked a finger down her cheek, trying to ignore the way she glared up at me.

"Oh, please. You aren't going to hurt me. I'm not made of glass." I shook my head and her glare turned into a pout. "Please? I'll sleep better if you're beside me."

"You mean you'll sleep better because you'll have a punching bag to kick in your sleep," I teased her.

"I won't, I swear." She reached for my hand and gave it a little tug. "Please, Liam. I need you."

Everything inside of me froze and I closed my eyes as I savored her words. Ah, fuck. I couldn't turn that down. I wasn't strong enough to deny her now. Muttering a curse, I opened my eyes. "Okay, baby. Okay."

She grinned sleepily up at me and scooted over before turning onto her right side to give me room. I was a lot bigger now than I'd been when we'd been together before. I wasn't the skinny drug addict I'd once been. With Linc Spencer's help, I'd gained thirty pounds of muscle, so I took up a hell of a lot more room than she did.

I toed-off my shoes and carefully dropped down onto the bed next to her. When I remained on my side, she pouted at me again and gave my shoulder a shove. Sighing, I rolled onto my back, trying not to jostle her too much. As soon as I was comfortable, she pounced on me. Her head landed on my chest, her arm going across my waist and her leg wrapped over both of mine.

The feel of having her in my arms once more, of holding her like that, was pure nirvana. It was almost overwhelming. Something in my chest clenched and my eyes began to sting. A lump filled my throat, so big that I couldn't have spoken even if my life had depended on it.

I wrapped my arm around her shoulders and pressed my lips to the top of her head, closing my eyes as I breathed in her clean scent. Fuck, this felt good. It was better than anything I'd ever felt before— ten times more powerful than any drug I'd ever done.

She yawned and cuddled against my chest even more. We lay like that for a long while, neither of us speaking. I didn't want this little slice of paradise to end.

Soon, the hell of a week I'd had started to catch up to me and my eyes began to drift closed, sleep slowly taking me as its prisoner. I was almost under when I heard Gabriella speak.

"Maybe I did dream that you told me you loved me," she murmured, as if she were talking to herself.

My eyes snapped open and I lifted my head so I could see her face better. Her eyes were no longer sleepy, but full of sadness. "What did you say?"

She grimaced. "You haven't said it again, so I'm pretty sure I was dreaming the part where you said you loved me."

My stomach dropped. Fuck, I was such an idiot.

I hadn't realized I had not told her I loved her since she'd first woken up. I rarely said it to anyone, even my sister, who was the only other person in the world I loved as much as Gabriella. I wasn't the type of guy to just blurt out how I felt. I bottled it up, kept it hidden.

During our relationship, I hadn't told her how I felt about her, not once. That didn't mean I hadn't loved her then. I had probably fallen for her the first time we had literally bumped into each other. I'd been such a pussy back then, hiding my love from her like a coward.

Even though I hadn't said the words, that didn't mean I hadn't shown her how I felt, especially in the last few days. I was trying to prove to her that she was my everything. To build up her trust in me and earn her love back. I realized right then that she needed the words more than anything else I could have offered her.

With my free hand, I grasped hold of her chin, lifting her head so that I could see her eyes. She looked so damned sad, so fucking lost. I couldn't stand that. She should never have that look on her beautiful face. Never. "You didn't dream it," I told her and brushed a kiss over each of her eyes. "I love you, little Brie. More than anything or anyone in the world. You are my everything. I know I haven't proved that, especially in the last few years, but I swear to you on all that I have that I will change it."

"Liam." She breathed my name, her chin trembling.

I lowered my head and kissed her lips tenderly. My body instantly reacted but I reined in my desire. She was hurt; there was no way in hell I was going to try and seduce her then and there. My dick didn't like that, though, and pressed painfully against the zipper of my jeans.

"I love you too, Liam."

The pain below my waist was quickly forgotten as those five small, yet incredibly powerful, words washed over me. I sucked in a deep breath, felt my eyes and throat stinging tears and quickly closed my eyes, savoring those words and this feeling of wonder.

How could she still love me after everything I'd put her through? After all that fucked-up shit that I'd thrown her way time after time? Her strength and love knew no limits if she was capable of loving me, especially after how I'd treated her when I'd waken up from my accident. I had so many regrets. So many damn regrets and no way to correct them.

"Ah, baby." I pressed my forehead against hers. "I don't know how you're able to love me after everything I've put you through, but I'm so fucking glad you do."

I felt her fingers stroking through my hair, holding me against her. "I've loved you from day one, Liam. Even when you didn't want my love, when you didn't want me, I loved you."

"I've always wanted you, Brie. Always."

A small sigh left her. "It didn't seem like it."

"I know and I'm sorry. You scared the living hell out of me, baby. Not much in this world scares me, but you did. So I ran in the opposite direction, yet you still seemed to like me despite that and I started pushing you away instead." I shook my head, remembering my stupidity. "When you hooked up with Axton, I nearly lost my mind."

Her brown eyes darkened with regret. "Axton and I never should have gotten together. All he wanted was a shield from his feelings for Emmie and I just wanted to forget about you. It didn't help. Even when I was with him, all I could think about was you. You were like a cancer eating away at my sanity. I hated it, and you, almost as much as I loved you."

There were those three magical words again. 'I love you.' It was scary how much three little words put together like that was so fucking powerful. They were able to ease the tightness in my chest, yet make my throat dry and choked all at the same time. I wanted to hear those damn words a thousand times a day.

"When you and Ax broke up, I tried to clean up my act and went after you. I seriously fucked that up that first time, though. I was high and stupid, and I figured if you had really wanted to be with me for more than just a hookup, you would have stuck around even after Ax interrupted us."

Gabriella's eyes narrowed. "It didn't feel like you wanted me to stick around. If anything, it seemed like you were kicking me out. After seeing you go through women like you did drugs, I thought that once was all you wanted." She bit into her bottom lip for a long moment before grimacing. "It's crazy, Liam. All that time we were together we never really talked about how we felt." I grimaced, knowing that she was right. Sure we had talked, but never actually about how we felt. At least I hadn't. "I loved you and I always thought that you loved me back, but that was about it. When we were over, I figured I'd just imagined your love. And then you had the accident. You woke up and made me leave. I thought for sure that you hated me."

I jerked as if she'd stabbed me. "No." It came out louder than I expected. "God, no. Brie, I loved you—*love* you. I will always love you. No one, not one fucking person, touches my heart like you do."

"I believe you," she whispered.

Relief surged through me. "Thank you."

We slipped back into quietness that was kind of peaceful. I held her as close as I dared, not wanting to hurt her. Her breathing was starting to even out and mine was trying to mimic hers. Sleep was ready to drag me under again when I felt her nails dig into my back and she lifted her head.

"Liam, will you tell me about that night?"

I lifted my lids, frowning down at her. "What night, baby?"

"That New Year's Eve. Before the accident." I started to shake my head, not wanting to remember that fucked-up night but her eyes turned pleading. "I know you went to my grandfather's house. He told me what he said to you."

Everything inside of me turned cold. I started to pull away, that old bastard's words echoing in my ears. Gabriella tightened her arm around my waist. "Please don't go. If you don't want to tell me, then that's fine. I just wanted to hear your side."

"Fuck, Brie." I closed my eyes. "Did he tell you the truth, or just his version of it?" I wouldn't have put it past the old man to have continued to try and keep us apart even from the grave.

She let out a shaky breath. "I think he told me the truth. It was weighing pretty heavily on him and he knew he wasn't going to live through another night. What he told me… It was why I was at the festival in the first place. I needed to see you. I wanted to confront you about it and see if we still stood a chance."

"I don't know what you want me to say, then." I lifted my lids and focused on the wall behind her, not sure I was strong enough to meet her gaze yet.

"I wanted to hear it come from you. But if you don't want to…"

I pressed a finger to her lips, efficiently shutting her up. Swallowing hard, I finally locked gazes with her, letting her see all the emotions roiling inside of me. She let out a small gasp and I started telling her the story she obviously was desperate to hear…

Nineteen Months Earlier

New York in December was a nice sight. With the snow falling, the lights were making each snowflake almost glisten. Connecticut was even better. Not that I would ever want to live there, but still, it was pretty. I wondered if next December I would get to share this with Marissa and Gabriella.

Fuck, I hoped so.

It had taken me two days to get up the nerve, two days since my release from rehab, but here I was. Driving my Ferrari up the long-ass driveway that belonged to the Moreitti family. I'd made a wild guess and figured that Gabriella was here with the old man rather than at the New York apartment or even back in California with Alexis. I knew she loved her grandfather and tried to spend holidays with him as often as possible.

Swallowing the nervous nausea trying to climb its way out of my throat, I turned off my car and looked up at Gabriella's childhood home. Unlike me, she had grown up in a privileged household. Her grandfather and aunt ran a multimillion-dollar company, representing some of Italy's most important fashion designers. I'd grown up on a farm for the most part, and even though it had been profitable at times, more often than not it hadn't been. Not until OtherWorld had hit it big and Wroth had put his money into making it one of Tennessee's biggest working farms.

Muttering a vicious curse, I climbed out of my Ferrari and took the steps to the front door two at a time. My hand was sweaty as I lifted it to ring the doorbell. The wind was starting to pick up and I pulled my winter coat around me a little tighter as I waited for someone to open the door.

Two minutes passed with no answer so I rang the doorbell again. No answer. "Ah, come on, Brie," I muttered to myself and pressed the doorbell twice more before lifting my fist to knock. "Don't be like this."

From inside the house, I finally heard someone yelling out for me to hold my horses. Seconds later the door was pulled open and an angry-eyed Luciano Moreitti stood there glaring daggers at me. From the first time Gabriella had introduced us, Luciano had made it very clear that he didn't think I was good enough for his favorite granddaughter. We'd been in agreement on that, but I was selfish enough not to give a fuck. I might not be good enough, probably never would be, but I wanted to be a part of her life for as long as she was willing to let me.

"What do you want?" Luciano snarled, tying his robe around him a little more firmly.

Had I woke him up? It wasn't even seven o'clock on New Year's Eve. Disappointment flooded through me as I realized that Gabriella probably wasn't there after all. "I'm looking for Gabriella." Her full name sounded unnatural on my tongue, but I knew her grandfather hated it when I called her Brie.

"She's out," he informed me with a pleased smirk on his face. "An old boyfriend took her off hours ago for a party of some sort. She told me not to wait up for her."

My disappointed turned to jealousy mixed with regret and self-hate. So, she had moved on. What the fuck had I been thinking that she would actually wait for me to clean my shit up? I'd lost her…

"She's been seeing William for weeks now," Luciano continued, looking so pleased with himself. I wanted to punch the bastard in the face, make him swallow a few teeth. "I think they reconnected almost as soon as she came back from California in October."

A new pain sliced through me. She'd kicked me out in October and I'd gone straight into rehab, hoping to find the real me without the drugs. I had with the help of my doctor, nurses, and Dallas. But I'd also realized that I wasn't me without Gabriella. I wanted her back, needed that girl more than anything else in the world. Without her I was nothing—less than nothing, really.

And she hadn't even missed me. She had been hooking up with her ex while I'd been detoxing, fighting the hell that was cravings and excruciating pain of going without drugs completely cold turkey for the first time in over a decade. Had she even thought about me? Or was she over me and glad to be through with our relationship?

"William asked me yesterday if he could marry her," the old man was saying now and I tuned in as everything inside of me went cold. "I suspect he will be asking her tonight at that party he's taking her to."

What? No. No, no, no. God, I couldn't handle that. My fiery little Italian goddess married to someone else? It would destroy me. She couldn't marry someone else, give herself to him completely like that, maybe even have kids with him.

I stumbled back, my knees threatening to buckle as the force of that reality robbed me of my strength. "No," I choked out. "She wouldn't."

The smug look on Luciano's face turned from smug to steel. "*Si*, she will. And you can't do a damned thing about it. She deserves the kind of life that William can and will give her. What kind of life would she have with you, rocker-boy? One full of wondering if you will slip up again and perhaps overdose on those drugs you love more than her?"

I opened my mouth, ready to defend myself, but quickly snapped it shut. He was right. I had always fallen back into old habits in the past. I didn't know if I was going to this time, but there was always that chance...

No. Not this time. I was never going down that road again. I wanted to be the man Gabriella could be proud of. A man deserving of her. "I love her more than anything else. I'm done with the drugs."

"So you say, but I don't believe you. Leave her alone, Bryant. Let her marry William. She's moved on, you should do the same." With that said, he stepped back and slammed the door in my face. Leaving me standing there. Broken.

I was numb the entire drive back to New York. I drove on autopilot through the snow-filled night as I replayed Luciano Moreitti's words over and over in my head.

Was he right? I didn't know and that was what was killing me.

The sound of a horn honking suddenly pulled me from my inner hell. Seconds later I was blinded by the headlights of a car that had drifted into my lane. I gripped my steering wheel and tried to turn away from the oncoming vehicle but it was too late. The sound of metal crunching filled my ears milliseconds before the force of the impact sent me flying through the windshield.

And then there was nothing but blackness, and for once in my life—peace.

The sound of Gabriella's broken sob jerked me back from the past and I looked down at her. She was openly crying, her face full of horror and pain. I pulled her closer and pressed a kiss to the top of her head. "I'm sorry," I whispered. "I shouldn't have told you the part about the accident."

"No," she whispered. "No, I'm glad you did. I always wondered what your last thought was before you were thrown from the car. Now I do. It was about me… wasn't it?"

I wiped away her tears, but they continued to fall, pushing the dagger in my heart a little deeper with each one. "Yes. You were the last thing that crossed my mind before it went completely blank."

She tried to sit up, but I tightened my arms around her, keeping her right where I wanted her. In my arms. "*Nonno* lied, Liam. I never hooked up with William." She rolled her eyes as she said the other man's name, making me relax a little. "He was my first boyfriend when I was a teenager and we never did more than kiss a few times. Even back then, *Nonno* had aspirations of me marrying him. That was never going to happen, though. He's a sniveling little momma's boy. You know I can't stand guys like that. I don't know why *Nonno* would even think I would want someone like that."

Relief filled me and I was able to breathe easier for the first time since Luciano had told me she was going to marry that William fucker. I'd had nightmares for months after my accident, but they hadn't been about the wreck that had come so close to killing me. No, it had been about Gabriella marrying her faceless William. "Thank God, Brie."

Her brows lifted. "Didn't you ever wonder why I hadn't married him when I kept chasing after you once you'd been released from the hospital?"

I shrugged. "I figured you were feeling guilty or something and that was why you wanted to be with me again. I couldn't do that to you if that was the case and I didn't have the balls to ask if it was or not. I knew I didn't deserve you. I was all kinds of wrong for you and I believed your grandfather when he said that you had moved on. So I kept pushing you away when what I really wanted to do was grab hold of you and never let go." I tightened my arms around her. "Fighting my need for you was a million times worse than fighting any craving for any drug."

"Oh, Liam." She shook her head, a sad smile on her beautiful face. "You're all kinds of perfect for me. You are the only man I've ever loved. Ever. I would have fought the entire world for us if I'd known that you loved me. I only need you. No one else matters."

I knew I shouldn't. She was still healing, but I couldn't help myself. I lowered my head and captured her lips in a hungry kiss. My hands lowered and cupped her perfect ass, pulling her against my throbbing body. Fuck, she tasted so damn good. Nothing had ever tasted as good as she did. Nothing. I wanted to devour her, to consume her so she was just as much a part of me as I wanted to be a part of her.

"Mm," she moaned and pressed against my chest, forcing me to pull back. She gave me a small grin, but there was pain mixed in with the passion in her eyes. "Easy there, rock star. I'm not unbreakable right now."

Regret washed through me and I quickly ran my hands over her, checking for any damage I might have done—and yeah, touching all of my favorite parts along the way. "I'm sorry, baby. Where does it hurt? Are you okay?"

"I'm fine, Liam. Just tender and sore." She snuggled against my chest and I folded her closer. "As soon as I'm a little better, you can do whatever you want to me. For now, just hold me while I sleep. Okay?"

"Yes, my little Brie. Okay."

"Liam?" she murmured sleepily.

"Yeah?"

"I love you."

My throat closed up with emotion and I had to clear my throat a few times before I could answer her. "I love you, too."

Chapter Twenty

Gabriella

Three weeks. That's how long the doctors kept me prisoner in the hospital. Three weeks of having to put up with regular visits from the Feds. Three weeks of dealing with my Aunt Carina, although Alexis did a hell of a job running interference for me. Three weeks of sitting on my ass doing nothing but walking the halls when the nurses told me to and watching movies on repeat. Liam being there every second of every day made it bearable, but I was ready to climb the walls by the time Dr. Schiller informed me I was ready to go. Now I was ready to dance, with all the excitement running through me.

Annabelle had sent my band home a few days after I'd woken up, but had the bus come back for me a few days ago. I was able to make the long trip back to Los Angeles in comfort since I wasn't allowed to fly yet. I wasn't alone, either. Liam was on the bus, of course, but so were Annabelle, Marissa and Wroth. Oh, and I couldn't forget the security guys. All three of them.

Emmie had insisted and all my objections had been vetoed by everyone around me. Apparently those three goons in suits were going to be a big part of my daily life now. At least until whoever had tried to kidnap Mia was found. I'd tried to argue, but Liam had put his foot down and said it was done. As much as I loved that man, I wasn't going to put up with him putting his foot down like that for much longer. I was starting to feel smothered by all the attention everyone was giving me.

Except for Liam. I soaked that shit up like it was a life-giving substance. For me, it was. I'd been deprived of him for far too long and I was definitely making up for it now. Still, I wasn't going to let him boss me around for much longer.

Whoever that stupid bitch was that had shot me had better be found soon. I didn't want the security staff, and I had no say over them. It was making me grumpy that I hadn't gotten my own way, but I did understand all the anxiety. So, I was mostly pouting instead of bitching like I would have done if I hadn't taken the situation so seriously.

"Ah, you are so cute when you push out that bottom lip like that." Annabelle laughed. She was sitting across from me on one of the couches. Her phone was in her hands and she was switching from answering text messages, to watching the movie that was on, to teasing me.

When I'd switched managers, it hadn't been something I'd chosen to do on the spur of the moment. For a while I'd felt like I was in a rut with Craig. He'd been getting more and more big-named clients and I'd felt like I was being pushed down his list of priorities. I'd met Annabelle and her brother, Noah, a few years ago and when I'd learned that she was taking on more clientele, I'd called her. We'd talked back and forth through emails for nearly a month about where I wanted to go next in my career and a few weeks later I'd signed on with her.

Since then we'd gotten to know each other a little better. I loved her personality. She was a take-no-bullshit type of chick but she wasn't a complete hard-ass. Her humor gave her an approachable vibe that I liked. She'd always been close-lipped about her family life, though. I only knew the bare necessities. She had a brother who had been in the country music business, but was now retired. He was married and had three kids. I'd never met any of them except the brother the first time I'd met Annabelle.

I wouldn't have been against getting to know her better on that scale, but she didn't seem to want that, and I respected her privacy.

Or at least, I had.

The moment Liam had told me that he'd grown up with Annabelle and her brother, my curiosity had spiked and now I was itching to know what was up with her need for so much privacy. Did she have some scary family secret or something? I had over a hundred questions I wanted immediate answers to.

Thankfully, I had Marissa sitting beside me to do some of the asking.

"How are Noah and Chelsea doing?" she asked, taking a sip from her mug of tea.

If I hadn't been watching, I might have missed the subtle tightening of Annabelle's face, or the way her shoulders tensed before she forcefully made herself relax and smile at Marissa. "They're good. Still arguing every day, still making up like rabbits every night."

Marissa's laugh was as bell-like as always and I instinctively moved closer to her, wanting to absorb as much of that sound as possible. What was it about this chick that made me want to make her laugh like that as often as possible? Damn, if she weren't Liam's sister I might have developed a girl-crush on her. "Yes, I remember that. I'm surprised they don't have more than three kids."

Annabelle's smile dimmed a little but she nodded. "They wanted more, but Chelsea had a cancer scare a while back and the doctors decided to do a full hysterectomy just to be safe."

"Oh, no. I'm so sorry to hear that. Is she okay now?"

Annabelle nodded. "She's fine now. Lucky her, she doesn't have to deal with a period ever again."

"So you have three nieces? Nephews? Both?" I couldn't help but ask.

"Both," Annabelle answered, her eyes turning back to her phone as she spoke. "Audrey, Ben...and Mieke is the oldest."

"Mieke? That's such a pretty name. How did they come up with that one?" Marissa asked with her always-present smile.

Annabelle shrugged. "I'm not sure. It's Dutch so I think it might have been a distant relative of ours or something."

"I'm hungry," Wroth called out in his scary-ass deep voice as he came out down the hall from the roosts. "Tell the driver to stop for something. I feel like having a burger."

"Yes, because this thing will fit through a drive-thru so easily." Annabelle rolled her eyes at the hulking guitarist, obviously not in the least scared of him as so many other people tended to be. "There's stuff in the fridge, a-hole. Make yourself a sandwich."

Wroth's dark eyes lit up with amusement. "I thought maybe I'd missed having you around a little, Annabelle. You've just proven me wrong."

She pressed her hand to her chest and pouted out her bottom lip. "I'm heartbroken, Niall."

"Anna-Banana still has a sassy mouth, I see," Liam grumbled as he came out of the bathroom dressed in fresh jeans and a shirt, his hair still damp from his shower. "Why haven't you found a man to cure you of that, I wonder?"

"Fuck off, dickhead," she muttered. Her jaw clenched as she continued to answer her text messages. "I don't need a man. They are nothing but trouble that I don't need nor want."

"Leave her alone, Li," Marissa scolded her brother.

"Ah, that's no fun," he grumbled as he scooped me up into his strong arms and sat down in my spot with me on his lap.

Liam tucked me against him and I cuddled close, closing my eyes as I enjoyed the clean, masculine scent of his neck. I felt his lips near my ear and shivered. Three weeks of being so close to this man without getting so much as a small taste of what I needed from him had been torture. As soon as we got back to my West Hollywood apartment, I was going to kick everyone out and ravage the sexy beast holding me. He had a thousand new muscles that I needed to explore with my hands, lips, and tongue.

Feeling my shiver, he grinned as he pressed his lips to my temple. "Soon," he murmured low enough so that only I could hear him.

I nearly moaned in anticipation. We were still a few hours out, damn it. I was ready to kick everyone off the bus and demand he do naughty things to me right then and there.

Instead, I pressed my head against his chest and closed my eyes, listening as Marissa, Wroth and Annabelle continued to talk. Before I knew it, I was drifting off to sleep, a feeling of safety and peace making my body go weak against the man who owned my soul.

Something tickling over my cheek woke me sometime later. I brushed it away and snuggled into my pillow a little more. The soft tickle came again and I blew out a frustrated breath as I turned my head away, trying to hang on to the remnants of sleep.

A deep, sexy chuckle filled my ears, producing goose bumps along my entire body. I cracked open an eye to look up at Liam who was lying beside me on the bed in the only bedroom aboard my tour bus. His face was relaxed, his eyes slightly bloodshot from sleep. Vaguely, I remembered him carrying me to bed and then climbing in beside me.

Stretching out my arms, I grabbed hold of his shoulder and tried to tug him toward me. Screw waiting for when we got to the apartment; I wanted him now.

Another deep chuckle left him and he captured my hands, kissing my palms. "Soon," he murmured with a wink. "Marissa woke me up a few minutes ago. We're nearly there, baby."

I pouted out my bottom lip. "Not even a little kiss?"

His blue eyes darkened. "Especially not a kiss. I'm barely holding on, little Brie. Don't tempt me." He lowered my hand, pressing it over his already-hard cock. It flexed against my palm and he closed his eyes, groaning. "See?"

"Yes," I breathed. "Soon. You promise?"

His eyes lifted enough to meet my gaze. "I swear on everything I love that it will be soon."

I felt the bus slowing down and grinned up at him. "Yay. Now let's go tell everyone to go away so we can have wild sex against my front door."

His cock flexed again at my suggestion and he grinned. "One thing at a time, baby. Wild sex isn't going to happen until we get the all-clear from your doctor. It's going to be slow and easy for a few more weeks."

"But..." I pouted up at him again. "But..."

Liam released my hands. Smacking me lightly on the ass, he stood. "None of that. Now, get your sexy ass out of bed so we can get out of here."

Sighing dramatically, I sat up and threw my legs over the side of the bed. "Spoilsport,"

"Yup. I'm not doing anything that might hurt you or set your recovery back." I got another wink before he opened the door and stepped through. Sticking his head back inside the bedroom, he frowned at me. "Come on, woman."

"Okay, okay." I stood and ran my fingers through my hair a few times to get some of the tangles out before following after him. As I walked through the bus, I realized that everyone else was already off, including the three security guys. Shrugging, I descended the stairs and stepped off the bus.

"Surprise!"

I nearly jumped out of my skin as I looked around at the people surrounding me. I wasn't outside my apartment, but in front of a house in Malibu. What the hell? At least twenty people stood on the lawn, including all of the members of OtherWorld and their wives and children. Emmie and the Demons were there with their families as well.

My eyes landed for a moment on Mia, who gave me a happy smile and a wave. Her mother had let her come to visit me several times in the last few weeks and we'd bonded. Waving back, I switched my gaze to the others around me. There was Linc Spencer and a few of the band members who I remembered had been touring with Liam over the summer. I spotted Alexis with Jordan and Jared. My aunt was there with a half-smile on her face. Even my own band was in attendance.

Never in a million years would I have thought that all of these people would come together like this—and for me, of all things. It boggled my mind, but melted my heart at the same time.

What was going on here? What were all these people doing here? And why weren't we home, where I wanted to be most in the world right then?

My eyes searched for and locked with Liam's. He was standing between Alexis and Natalie Cutter. His earlier grin was gone, replaced with what looked like anxiety. "I thought we were going home," I muttered.

He shrugged, looking even more nervous than he had just a second before. "We are."

My brows lifted toward the sky. "What are you talking about, Liam?"

He stepped aside and for the first time I saw the 'For Sale' sign with some older man's picture—I assumed the realtor—on the front lawn. A red and white sign was now over the realtor's face, proclaiming the place 'Sold'. My gaze went to the house. From the outside, it was beautiful. Two stories, painted in dark brown with hunter green shutters. I instantly fell in love with it. Especially when I realized what street we were on.

Alexis lived only a few houses down.

"I thought we needed a new start in a house that was ours," Liam told me. "Natalie and Emmie have been working their asses off for the last three weeks, getting this done for me. Do you like it?"

My throat was so choked up with emotion that I couldn't immediately answer him. Taking my silence as a negative, his face fell a little. "If it's not what you want we can find something better," he rushed to assure me.

I launched myself at him to shut him up. "I love it," I whispered. "Thank you. I love you."

His arms tightened around my waist, holding me against him like a vice. I felt a shudder rake his body. "I love you more."

A small laugh escaped me. "Not possible."

His lips brushed over my forehead as he pulled back enough to look down at me. "Wanna bet?" Before I could even open my mouth to tease him, he was letting go of my waist and grasping hold of my hands as he knelt on his good leg before me.

My heart stopped, my breath freezing in my lungs. *Oh, my God!* my brain shouted as my eyes burned with the tears that tried to blind me. Surprise mixed with disbelief and overwhelming joy rocked through me and I couldn't move, couldn't even blink as I looked down at him.

I watched through my tears as he swallowed hard. I thought maybe Natalie put something in his hand, but I couldn't be sure because my focus was completely on Liam. "I've loved you from the moment I set eyes on you. You've made me a stronger, better man and I will strive to always be someone you will be proud to call your own. I want to be beside you every day for the rest of my life." His voice cracked and he swallowed roughly again. "Will you let me, little Brie?"

I could feel everyone's eyes boring into me as I stood there, completely dumbfounded by what was happening. I'd wanted this for so long, had been determined that this was exactly what I wanted. But I'd thought that I would be the one to have to move us in that direction.

This? I wouldn't have expected this in a million years. I couldn't believe Liam was doing this, putting himself out there like that in front of his friends in such a vulnerable way. It just showed me once again how much he had changed and I couldn't help falling that much more in love with him.

Still unable to speak, barely able to see through my tears, I nodded my head joyously at him. I felt him slide a ring onto my finger before he was on his feet and I was in his arms, sobbing so hard that my still slightly sore chest ached. Liam pressed his lips to my ear, telling me over and over again that he loved me. I felt something damp on my neck and realized that he was crying too.

My arms tightened around his neck and I buried myself against him as much as humanly possible. "I love you," I croaked out. "I love you so much."

Liam

It took hours before everyone finally left. I was exhausted so I knew Gabriella had to be as well. She'd gone upstairs as soon as our last guest had left ten minutes before and I'd started cleaning up the disaster our newly furbished home had become.

I had picked up all the paper plates and empty cups in a trash bag before I decided to let the housekeeper that Natalie had hired for us deal with the rest the next day. I wanted a shower and the new bed Annabelle had picked out with the help of Marissa and Alexis. The inside of the house was just as perfect as the outside, or so Gabriella had assured me when I'd shown her around. Of course it was my first time seeing everything up close and personal rather than just in pictures. From the evidence of my new home, I had to admit that between Emmie, Natalie, and Annabelle, I figured they could have ruled the world with ease.

Shaking my head at that thought, I opened the door to the master bedroom. From our connecting bathroom I could hear the water still running for Gabriella's shower. Just thinking of my girl standing under the stream of steaming water, touching herself as she washed, caused my body to instantly wake up. Grinning, I pulled my shirt over my head on my way into the bathroom, before quickly taking care of the rest of my clothes.

The bathroom was full of steam as I entered and I could barely make out the shape of the little Italian goddess as she sang softly to herself and swayed those damn amazing hips to the rhythm in her head. If I'd still been wearing my jeans, I knew I'd have hurt myself with the way my dick went from semi-hard to full attention in less than a second. My mouth went dry as I stood there watching her dancing under the spray of the shower.

It was sweet torture to watch her like this. I'd been aching for her for far too long and the need in my body was trying to block out every rational thought my brain was trying to process right then. I clenched my jaw, trying to rein my demanding body in. It was a difficult struggle, though. The last time I'd had sex was with the little goddess behind the shower door.

Twenty-two months.

That was how long it had been since I'd last had sex. That was how long it had been since I'd been deep inside of my girl. It was probably hard to believe, but it was the truth. There had been plenty of opportunities to hook up with any number of chicks—I was a fucking rock star, after all, and girls constantly threw themselves at me—problem was, I hadn't been interested. Not one of those chicks had tempted me.

Yet just the thought of the water running over Gabriella, touching her in all the places I wanted to touch her, turned me into a motherfucking Neanderthal. I couldn't think past how quickly it would take me to slide deep into her tight little body.

Groaning, I opened the shower door. Gabriella stopped singing, but her hips continued swaying to whatever tune was playing in her head. She grinned up at me and pulled me into the shower with her. I didn't even see the angry scar on her chest as her wet breasts rubbed over my chest while she wrapped her arms around my waist and ran her fingers up and down my back. To me, that fucking scar wasn't even there. She was alive and perfect. That was all that mattered. Shivering, I pulled her closer and lowered my head.

The damn little tease turned her head away and my lips landed on her jaw. I reached out, my hands gripping her perfect ass and trailed kisses down her neck until I reached the tender flesh where neck met shoulder. Sinking my teeth in, I heard her cry out with pleasure and knew that that had been exactly what she had wanted.

"Don't tease me," I growled against her ear. "Give me your lips."

She looked up at me through damp lashes. "Tell me you love me first," she commanded.

"I love you. I adore you. I fucking need you." I tightened my hold on her ass and lifted her a few inches off the tiled shower floor. Her delighted gasp filled my ears as my throbbing dick brushed over the outer lips of her wet pussy. "Now let me have your mouth."

She pouted her lips at me and I lowered my head, capturing that sassy mouth. Her taste exploded on my tongue, making my entire body weak with need. I backed up until I felt the bench touching my calves and lowered to the stone seat. Her legs wrapped around my waist, opening her sweet-scented pussy up for me. My dick jerked, wanting inside that hot little haven.

Muttering a curse, I ended the kiss and sucked in one deep breath after another. I needed to slow down. I'd told her earlier that there would be no rough sex until the doctor said she was completely healed. There was no way in hell I was going to risk hurting her.

Gabriella pressed her forehead to mine, breathing just as erratically as I was. "Please," she whimpered. "Please, Liam. I need you inside of me."

I gritted my teeth as I tried to fight for control over my damn body. "Is it okay? Are you still on the pill?" She nodded her head quickly and I nearly lost my mind. "Fuck," I growled as I reached between us and grasped hold of my pulsing dick. "Ah, fuck." I could feel the heat radiating from her pussy even before I brushed the tip over her drenched slit.

She bit her lip and half closed her eyes as she watched me position my dick at her entrance. With my free hand, I spread her lips wide and brushed my thumb over her clit, making her gasp and arch her back, opening up her pussy even more for me. Carefully, I pushed up into her. My eyes rolled back into my head as her tight walls sucked me in. Her wetness made the first thrust glide smoothly, but she was still as tight as an undersized glove.

When I was in as far as her little body would let me, I lowered my head and buried my face in the valley between her luscious tits, pressing kisses to her scar. Fucking hell. I could have died a happy man right then. I had everything I wanted, everything I fucking needed, right there, holding onto me just as tightly as I was holding onto her.

This was the ultimate high. This was paradise.

Gabriella

I picked up my water glass and took a sip as I glared across the table at Emmie. "Why not?" I demanded with a pout.

Big, green eyes rolled at me. "Because you're eight months pregnant, that's why. You should rest, not watch after an eight-year-old."

"But I'll be good, Momma," Mia promised, giving her mother the same pout that I was still sporting. "Please? I'll be a good girl and help Aunt Gabs if she needs anything? Please? Pretty, pretty please?" When it didn't look like Emmie was going to relent, Mia played her last card. "Roger will be there. He can stay in the extra guest room."

I glanced over Emmie's shoulder at the hulking guard sitting inconspicuously at a neighboring table. Roger was more or less Mia's shadow these days. The poor little girl couldn't even go outside in her own backyard without Roger standing over her. I understood Emmie's reasoning, especially after what had happened with not just the attempted kidnapping, but what had come later. I still had nightmares about both those terrible days so I knew that Emmie probably did too.

I also knew how smothered Mia felt. She told me all the time how much she wished she was a normal little girl, from a normal family. Mia loved her mother and father, and she would never have asked for someone else to be her parents; she simply wished they were ordinary people, with ordinary jobs.

In the last three years, the bond that Mia and I had developed after the attempted kidnapping had strengthened. I had Emmie to thank for that—and yeah, having a reason to be thankful for Emmie Armstrong still messed with my head a little—but I did. She'd let my relationship with Mia develop. Hadn't stood in the way when the two of us needed to talk about that terrifying night. She'd even let Mia spend a few nights with me over the years.

Through my bonding with Mia, Emmie and I had been able to find a workable middle ground as well. I wasn't going to go as far as to say we were best friends, but we were somewhat friends. Especially since Liam had admitted to never having feelings for Emmie. I'd nearly slapped his beautifully masculine face for setting that particular ruse up. Emmie and I had put it behind us, though, and I'd even apologized for the whole 'lying about sleeping with her husband' thing. It was water under the bridge now. We had lunch together at least once a month, sometimes with Layla and the other Demons' wives, or with Alexis or Annabelle and if Marissa was in town she always joined us.

The first time one of the paps had spotted me having a meal with Emmie, they had sold the picture for a small fortune and the article had been titled "IS THE END COMING?" like the two of us eating together was the sign of an apocalypse or some crazy shit. I'd laughed my ass off while reading that stupid piece of trash. Really? Was it so hard for people to imagine that Emmie and I could sit down at a table and talk without killing each other?

Okay, so maybe it was a little farfetched for people to imagine that, especially given our history. But things change and so do people. Liam had proven that to me over and over again in the last three years.

Emmie blew out a frustrated breath. "Okay. Compromise with me here, ladies. Mia can spend tomorrow night with you, Gabriella, *if* she does well on her reading test tomorrow morning."

I glanced at Mia, who was frowning at her mother. "You're trying to extort good grades out of me?"

"You got a C on your last test, Mia. You didn't even try. Your teacher said you just rushed through it and then turned the test over and started drawing on the back. Get an A tomorrow and you can have your sleepover at Gabriella's." Emmie sounded stern but reasonable and because I knew the responsible thing to do was back her up, I nodded at Mia.

"You get an A and we'll go shopping and have a sleepover," I promised her. "But if you get anything lower, we have to wait until next weekend."

Mia's lip pouted out even more for a moment before she blew out a dramatic sigh and gave in. "Okay. I will strive for an A. But only because I want to sleep over at Aunt Gabs."

Emmie muttered something under her breath, causing Mia to roll her eyes before she picked up the rest of her grilled cheese sandwich.

Our late lunch date ended a short time later and I hugged Mia goodbye before climbing into the back of the waiting Lincoln Navigator. My own personal bodyguard was behind the wheel and ready to drive me back to the house in Malibu. Over the years, I'd been able to talk Liam down from three goons in a suit to just one since the threat of imminent danger was no longer an issue. I only put up with the one because I knew how much my husband worried when I left the house without him.

I leaned my head back and rubbed a hand over my very distended stomach, a happy smile on my face. It was hard to believe that Liam was my husband, even after two and a half years of marriage. It felt surreal that I had everything I'd always wanted but thought I would never have. Sometimes I thought it was all a dream and then I would rub my fingers over the scar on my chest and remind myself that it really was possible to have it all.

My driveway was full of vehicles that didn't belong to me when Miles, my driver/bodyguard pulled to a stop. Five rockers were standing on the front lawn with my husband, obviously getting ready to leave. Zander, Devlin, Axton, Jesse, and Nik had come over to do some song-writing before both bands got back into the studios in a few weeks. Wroth was noticeably absent, but he only came to the West Coast when he had—or Marissa had—a hankering to see her brother.

On Nik's shoulders was Jagger, who was laughing down at Axton's son, Cannon. The younger little rocker was rolling around on the grass and I knew Dallas was going to be less than thrilled when she saw the grass stains on her son's white shirt.

Not waiting for Miles to open the door for me, I stepped out of the Navigator. Pulling my shirt down over my baby bump, I started toward the six men. All eyes turned to me as I approached, but I had eyes for only one man. Liam stepped forward to meet me, wrapping his strong arms around my waist tenderly and dropping a gentle kiss on my lips.

"Mm," he growled. "You taste good."

I licked my bottom lip, savoring his taste on my tongue. "You too, rock star."

"Well, I think that's our cue to head home." Axton laughed and picked his son up like a sack of potatoes, tossing the adorable little guy over his shoulder. "Tell Jags bye, Cannon."

Cannon wiggled around so he could see his dad's face and pouted his full lips at him, having obviously inherited that particular trait from his gorgeous mother. "I don't want to. Can't we stay and play a little longer? Oh, oh. Can I sleep over at Jagger's? Please, Daddy? Please?"

"Momma said the next time I came home without you I would be sleeping in your bed." Cannon's chin wobbled and Axton shook his head. "Not tonight, little dude. Maybe Momma will say yes tomorrow since it's Friday."

Nik chuckled, tightening his hold on Jagger's ankles. "Don't worry, Cannon. I'm sure we can work something out. Right, Jags?" Always the quiet one, Jagger gave a simple yet completely serious nod. "Right. Well, we're heading home. See you guys tomorrow."

I nearly groaned at that. They were going to take over my house again? Weren't they done yet? It had been two weeks now. I wanted all those freaking men out of my house.

As if he could read my mind, Liam pressed a kiss to my ear. "We'll be over at Nik's tomorrow."

I let out a relieved sigh and leaned into him as we said goodbye to everyone. Jesse and Nik got into the same vehicle after Jagger was secured in his booster seat. Devlin drove off behind Zander, leaving Axton and Cannon the last of our guests. Ax stuck his hand out his window as he drove off, waving, and I lifted my hand to wave back. "Tell Dallas I said hello," I called after him.

"You could call her and tell her yourself," he called back with a smirk.

If his son hadn't been in the car, I probably would have shot him the finger, but I refrained just in time. Like Emmie and me, Dallas and I had a better relationship these days as well. By 'better' I meant she was over the fact that I'd once had a relationship with her husband and I was content to be on speaking terms with her that didn't include us calling each other nasty names. It was definitely a step higher than our email 'friendship' from a few years before.

Once his car was out of sight, I turned in Liam's arms. "Been getting into trouble while I was out?"

"Nope. I was a good boy, Momma." That sexy grin that never failed to get my panties wet spread over his face, making me a little weak in the knees. Large hands cupped the swell of my belly. "What about this little guy? Did he give you any problems?"

I rubbed my hand over my stomach. "*She* has been just fine," I assured him. The truth was, we didn't know what we were having. Both of us had wanted to wait and be surprised when our baby arrived. I didn't care what we were having, but I loved teasing Liam about it. If he said 'he' then I said 'she'. If he said 'she' then I always said 'he'. It drove him nuts.

Releasing a snort of laughter, Liam bent slightly and swept me up in his arms. Surprised, I let out a shriek as he started climbing the steps to the porch. "Liam!" I tried to wiggle free. "Stop. Put me down. Please, I weigh a ton and I don't want you to hurt your leg."

He tightened his arms around me and continued to walk with my heavy weight not seeming to bother him in the least. "You barely weigh anything, woman. Now sit still before you cause me to drop you."

I glowered up at him but quit struggling for freedom. Once we were in the house, I figured he would set me down, but he started climbing the stairs to the second floor instead. "Liam, please. Your leg."

He rolled his blue eyes at me. "My leg is fine, little Brie. I'm good, sweetheart. Now stop. I'm trying to be romantic here, okay?"

"Sorry." I bit my lip to keep from laughing. "Please continue."

I thought he was going to take me to our room but he bypassed it and went to the room directly across from it. The nursery.

Carefully, he shifted me so he could deal with the door without putting me down and used his foot to push the door all the way open. Once we were over the threshold, he set me on my feet and reached for the light switch.

I blinked several times before my eyes adjusted to the light and when I realized what I was seeing, my knees went weak. Strong arms wrapped around my waist, pulling me against his strong body so that I wouldn't fall. Happy tears fell freely from my eyes as I glanced around the finished nursery.

It hadn't even been touched when I'd left that morning. I'd been procrastinating on setting everything up and had only picked out the paint I'd wanted for the baby's room the week before. Now the walls were all painted along with the rock-n-roll bears in their leather jackets, guitars, and drumsticks border that I'd fallen in love with perfectly in place. A beautiful crib had been set up along with a changing table already fully equipped with everything we would need. A rocker sat by the crib and, in the corner, a toy chest already brimming with toys that were suitable for either a boy or a girl.

Wiping at my tears with the back of my hand, I turned my wet eyes on Liam. "How?"

He grinned down at me. "There was very little music-writing getting done in this house today, baby. Our friends helped me. Do you like it?"

I nodded my head joyfully. "Yes. I love it. It's perfect. Thank you. This is what I was dreaming of for the baby. You did good, Daddy."

As they always did when I called him that, Liam's eyes brightened suspiciously and he swallowed hard a few times before speaking. "I wanted to surprise you."

"You definitely did that."

His grin returned and he released my waist, taking the hem of my shirt with him as he lifted his hands. In one smooth move, my shirt was over my head, leaving me standing there in my black maternity leggings and one of the new bras I'd had to buy recently because my breasts were already a cup-size bigger.

Liquid heat flooded my pussy at the look in Liam's blue eyes as he stared down at me. One large, calloused hand cupped my breast through the material of my cotton bra. "You are the most beautiful thing I have ever set eyes on. How did I get so fucking lucky?"

I gasped as he rubbed his thumb over my already diamond-hard nipple. "You deserve this," I assured him before moaning in pure pleasure as he pinched my nipple between his thumb and forefinger. My nipples had gotten so sensitive during this pregnancy that I knew he could make me come just by continuing what he was doing. He tugged on the nipple, making me pant with need. "I love you, Liam. We deserve this."

He dropped to his knees in front of me. For a split second I worried about him aggravating his leg, but that was quickly thrown from my mind when he pressed his lips just under my belly button. "I love you, little Brie. More than anything in the world. You are my everything. Forever will never be long enough to be with you. I would walk through hell and back just to keep you beside me for eternity."

I combed my fingers through his hair as tears once again poured from my eyes. "Stop making me cry," I whispered.

His jaw tightened. "I swear to you that happy tears are all that you'll ever cry again."

A small smile teased at my lips. "You can't promise that, Liam. There are going to be times when I get sad or lost and I'm going to cry. There will be times when I ugly-cry all over the place. And that's okay, because I know you'll always be right here to hold me and make it all better for me."

"Damn straight I will be."

I laughed at the stern expression on his face. "*Dio*, I love you."

"I love you more," he murmured.

"Not possible," I teased, knowing exactly how he would react.

"Wanna bet?" He tugged me down onto the floor. "Let's see, yeah?"

And like he knew I would, I let him try to prove he loved me more.

PLAYLIST

"The Ever" by Red
"Flashlight" by Jesse J
"Life is Beautiful" by Sixx A. M.
"Drunk Enough" by Angels Fall
"Girl With Gold Eyes" by Sixx A.M.
"The Past" by Sevendust (ft. Chris Daughtry)
"Love Me Til It Hurts" by Papa Roach
"Part That's Holding On" by Red
"Bad Girls World" by Halestorm
"Let Your Tears Fall" by Kelly Clarkson
"My Heart Is Broken" by Evanescence
"Always" by Killswitch Engage
"The Last Goodbye" by David Cook
"The Humble River" by Puscifer
"Hit The Ground" by Hinder

Acknowledgements

From the beginning I've had a handful of people who wanted to know more about Gabriella Moreitti. They saw the good in her long before I ever could. They begged and pleaded for her story and after several books, she finally spoke to me. It wasn't easy getting inside of her head so this book was definitely a difficult one for me to write. Still, I want to thank all of the fans who championed for Gabriella's happily ever after. It took me a while, but I finally saw the light.

Special thanks to everyone who helped make this book beautiful for you: Shawna Kruse and her amazing talent behind a camera. Lance Jones and Jurnee Lane for gracing the cover. Rachel Mizer for her lovely touch to the cover itself. And especially to Lorelei Logsdon who makes sense of my ramblings and cleans it all up so you have an actual book to read.

As always I want to take a moment to thank my husband, Mike Browning, and our three demon spawn for putting up with me throughout the creation of all these books. Thank you for putting up with all my mood swings and craziness. I love you all to the moon and back. Always.

MORE BY TERRI ANNE BROWNING

THE ROCKER SERIES
Book 1: The Rocker Who Holds Me
Book 2: The Rocker Who Savors Me
Book 3: The Rocker Who Needs Me
Book 4: The Rocker Who Loves Me
Book 5: The Rocker Who Holds Her
Book 6: The Rockers' Babies
Book 7: The Rocker Who Wants Me
Book 8: The Rocker Who Cherishes Me
Book 9: The Rocker Who Shatters Me
Book 10: The Rocker Who Hates Me

THE ANGELS SERIES
Book 1: Angel's Halo
Book 2: Entangled
Book 3: Guardian Angel

THE LUCY AND HARRIS SERIES
Book 1: Catching Lucy

Reckless With Their Hearts
Reese: A Safe Haven Novella

Follow Terri Anne Browning
www.facebook.com/writerchic27
www.terriannebrowning.com
Twitter@AuthorTERRIANNE

Turn the page for a sneak peek into Protect Me by Kathy-Jo Reinhart.
Available now.

PROTECT ME
(Oakville Series: Book Three)

By:
Kathy-Jo Reinhart

PROLOGUE

~*Paul*~

"Well, which one do you guys think she'll like?" I question Becky and Kyle. We are all gazing down at a jewelry tray full of engagement rings. It took a lot of begging on my part, but I was able to convince my best friend and one of Holly's best friends to come with me today. I understand Becky's hesitation in coming along. She hasn't known Holly for very long and wasn't sure she'd be the best choice to help me choose her engagement ring. Kyle, however, has no excuse. We've been friends for too long. He tried to pull the I-just-had-a-baby card with me. That shit didn't work. Amber just had a baby, not him.

Somehow, I was finally able to convince them both. I need this ring today. Amber and Cody are coming home from the hospital later this afternoon and Holly being Holly is throwing a little welcome home party at their house. All of the people we love will be there. Most people would propose in a quiet and romantic setting, but I know my girl. After being alone for such a long time, Holly and I never imagined we'd find each other, let alone a group of friends who are more like a family. So, asking her to be my wife in front of all the special people in our lives will be her idea of perfect. I have to admit, I kinda think it's perfect, too. That's not to say I'm not nervous as hell, though. Looking down at the shiny diamond rings, my throat goes dry and my heart beats rampantly in my chest. Why? I don't know. I'm positive she'll say yes, so why am I still so fucking nervous?

"Hello? Earth to Paul. You asked us a question then zoned out on us, dumbass. Did you even hear what Becky said?" Kyle teases. He knows I've wanted to do this since the second my eyes landed on Holly. I never believed in that whole "love at first sight" bullshit until I saw her. Although, maybe it was more lust at first sight and love at first sound. Holly is a knockout, there's no doubt about it, but I think it was her take-no-shit attitude that made me fall for her. She is definitely one spunky ass redhead. Give her any shit and she will light your ass up. Though, I need to snap out of it and pay attention. This is important. My doll-face deserves the perfect ring.

"Sorry, Becky. I'm a little nervous," I admit. They both gawk at me like I've lost my mind, but who wouldn't be a little nervous in this situation? Hopefully they don't see just how nervous I really am. It has taken a long time for me to feel like I deserve to be happy at all, let alone loved by such an amazing woman. For a while, before I met Kyle, I was so fucked up in the head, I didn't care whether I lived or died. I think I would've actually preferred death.

"I remember when I was doing this and a certain someone was teasing the shit out of me for being nervous. What was it you said? Oh, yeah...'being nervous is for pussies, of course she's gonna say yes'," Kyle playfully says between chuckles. Even Becky joins in and giggles. "At least now you get it." I'm so glad they're finding this all so amusing.

"Yes, I get it assnugget. Now, can you stop busting my balls and help me?" I joke and add a brotherly slap to the back of his head. Kyle winces in pain and steps out of slapping range. Okay, maybe it was a little harder than a brotherly slap. Becky looks between the both of us, the corners of her mouth threatening a smile.

"Wow." She shakes her head. "I have no idea why the two of you would be nervous about asking two beautiful, smart, and very mature women to marry you," Becky states sarcastically. She turns so she's facing us both with her hands resting on her hips. In this moment, I can see Holly has turned this sweet and quiet girl into her little sarcastic sidekick. The world is not prepared for two of them. "Can you two stop acting like ten year olds long enough to do what we came to do? I have a party to help with." She smiles at the both of us and goes back to examining the rings in front of her.

This is a lot harder than I thought it would be. Holly isn't really a girly girl. Buying her some big, flashy diamond won't impress her in the least. I need to find something special. Everyone has a diamond engagement ring, she would have something different. Something original.

"Do you have any amethyst engagement rings?" I question the eager salesgirl. Ever since she began helping us, she's hung on every word, overacting like she really gives a damn about helping me and not just the huge commission at the end of the sale. The minute my question registers with her, all that changes. Her face tenses. The free, easy smile she wore minutes ago is gone, replaced with a hard, forced one.

"We do have amethyst rings, but traditional engagement rings are diamond. Amethyst is a much cheaper stone," she states a little too prissy for my taste. Oh, I see, she's one of those types. The total opposite of Holly. She's the girl who has to have a ring that costs more than a house. "If it's cheap you're looking for, maybe you're in the wrong place." This time, her voice has a bite to it. Her eyes scan me from head to toe, trying to determine whether I even have the means to be in this expensive store. She starts to put the tray of rings back into the display case. My body begins to tense up as sweat builds on my forehead. Her tone and the fact that she's insinuating I should go somewhere else because I don't want a diamond engagement ring pisses me off.

I glance to my right and find a massive grin on Kyle's face. He's trying his damnedest not to laugh, which fuels my anger. Seeing my expression, he raises his chin in Becky's direction. Before I can fully turn to my left to see what he's laughing at, I hear it. Becky is pissed off. I think she's more pissed at this bitch than I am. I've only seen her mad once, when Leena drugged Kyle and made everyone think she and Kyle slept together. The way she's acting right now, you'd think this girl just insulted her and not me. Her voice is calm, but you can feel the anger radiating off her. When I finally get a glimpse of her face, even I'm a little scared. Her nostrils are flaring and there's a vein raised on the side of her forehead. She just plain looks badass. I need to remember not to get on this girl's bad side — ever.

"This may come as a shock to you, but not every woman wants or even likes the traditional diamond engagement rings. The girl this ring is for isn't some superficial, prissy, materialistic Barbie Doll." She pauses, taking a deep breath, most likely trying to calm herself down. She clenches her hands so tightly at her sides, the knuckles are turning white. "Another little known fact: just because someone doesn't buy the most expensive thing in the store doesn't mean they can't afford to." The salesgirl just stands there with her mouth hanging open and eyes wide. Becky searches the store. Something catches her eye and a sinister smirk sprouts on her lips. "You get paid on commission, correct?" The stunned salesgirl nods. "That gentleman over there in the black suit, is he your boss?" Becky points to the well-dressed man sitting behind the counter at a desk. Now the salesgirl looks nervous as she nods her head slowly. Her bottom lip is trembling, like she's going to burst into tears at any second. "Well, then, this is really going to suck for you, sweetheart. Maybe next time you'll think before you open your mouth," Becky warns as she struts toward the man in the suite.

Kyle bursts out laughing. He's doubled over, almost as if he were in pain. When he straightens up, there are tears running down his cheeks. Still standing frozen, with her mouth gaping open in disbelief, the salesgirl watches Becky introduce herself to the manager of the store. Holy shit! I don't know whether to be scared or impressed by this side of Becky we've never seen before. I never imagined she could be such a bitch. Not that this girl doesn't deserve whatever is about to happen to her — she most definitely does.

We all stand quiet and still, watching Becky and the manager talk. She points to me and the manager looks over, nods, and smiles. As soon as the conversation gets to the good part, you can see it. He glances at the now trembling girl behind the counter. They both begin to walk over to us. I glance over at the salesgirl, who now resembles a frightened caged animal. The manager stands in front of the girl while Becky eagerly watches, awaiting the girl's fate.

"We'll discuss this later, Natasha. For now, the bathrooms and break room need a good cleaning," he instructs. Natasha's expression is priceless. I don't even know how I would describe it. Shock. Horror. Anger. All of them seem to cross her face. It's quite amusing. Finally, she turns on her heels and stomps off toward the back of the store. I notice the very pleased grin plastered on Becky's face while Kyle tries to control his laughter.

"My name is Charles. Please excuse my sister. She can be a real snob sometimes," he apologizes. "How may I help you?" I explain what I'm looking for and he leads us to another counter with nothing but amethyst rings. This is more like it, more like my Holly — beautiful and unique. It doesn't take long to find the perfect ring. A large pear shaped amethyst stone sits atop a thick platinum band with diamonds in the shape of angel wings resting on each side. It's the most unique and beautiful ring I've ever seen and it just screams Holly.

As we drive back to Kyle's, I can't help but think back on my life. Never did I think I'd live past twenty-five, not with the way I went through booze, drugs, and women. One of them was sure to be the death of me at some point. The fact that I actually allowed myself to fall in love amazes me the most. That's most definitely the one thing I swore I would never let happen. I was too broken. Too lost. Too guilty. Nothing good could come from me being in love, or so I thought.

~Holly~

Where the hell is Becky? She promised she'd be here to help me get this little "Welcome Home" party together for Amber and the baby. Though…I mainly want her here so she and Clark are around one another. There are some serious sparks between those two, but neither of them seem to want to do anything about it. So, I'm taking it upon myself to give them a little push.

"Holly, where do you want me to layout all of the food?" Clark questions, walking out of the kitchen. When he sees me struggling to blow up the extra-large blue balloons, he laughs. Filling the house with a hundred or so baby blue balloons seemed like a great idea when I was at the party store yesterday. Today, not so much. I'm dizzy and out of breath and I've only managed to completely inflate five. This sucks. Plopping down on the couch, I release the half-filled balloon from my fingers and watch it fly through the living room.

"This is useless. I'll never get these blown up before everyone gets here." Clark sits beside me as he tries to contain his laughter.

"I have one of those disposable helium tanks at the house. It was left over from Skylar's last birthday party. Would you like me to run home and grab it?" *He hasn't left yet?* I give him a 'what the fuck are you waiting for?' look. Quickly, he's on his feet and heading for the door. I don't fail to notice his laughter has returned. This is what it must feel like to have annoying little brothers. These boys just love to push my buttons. But I love them anyway. They're the only family I have.

While I wait, I decide to hang the "Welcome Home" banner. As I start to climb the ladder, Paul and Becky walk in. That's strange. What are they doing together? Becky looks nervous and Paul is hiding something. I'm pretty damn good at reading people. Except for one. Somehow, he fooled me, but that's all in the past now.

"Nice of you to finally show up to help," I tease them.

"Sorry, doll-face. I needed Kyle and Becky's help with something. No, I won't tell you what. It's a surprise," he explains as he kisses my forehead. When he pulls away, there's a shit-eating grin on his face. He's up to something and I want to know what it is. I know there's no use in pushing. Paul is the master of keeping a surprise, a surprise.

When Clark gets back, I need you to help him get the food ready," I tell Becky, not giving her a chance to protest. As if on cue, Clark comes through the front door. As soon as his eyes land on Becky, his whole face lights up. "Clark, Becky can help you with the food and Paul can help me with the rest of the decorations." He nods and they both walk into the kitchen. Paul looks at me and smiles, shaking his head. He knows exactly what I'm trying to do.

It didn't take long before Angel, Chelsie, Marcus, Taryn, and their boys showed up. Once I gave them all something to do, we finished setting up in no time. Beasley, Marty, and Anna arrived just as Kyle called saying they were five minutes away.

I want this to be memorable for both Kyle and Amber. They've both been through more shit than any two people should have to. No one was sure this day would be possible after she lost the triplets. It wasn't just the two of them who were affected by it either. We all were. We are all family. Maybe not all by blood, but family all the same. When one of us hurts, we all do. This group pulled together to do everything possible to help her get this baby here, safe and sound.

As soon as we hear Kyle's truck pull up the drive, we all rush to the door. You'd think we hadn't seen baby Cody yet. The nurses had to kick us out more than once. Since he's the first baby in our group, it's almost as if he belongs to us all. I can't wait to be called Aunt Holly. This little boy will be so spoiled. Not only by his parents, but every single one of us. His nursery is already overflowing with clothes and toys.

"I should've known you'd throw me a party. There's no way you could pass up the opportunity," Amber jokes as she hugs me tight.

"Don't flatter yourself. I'm throwing this party for Cody, not you," I tell her as I take the car seat from Kyle and head for the house. I hear Amber mumble bitch under her breath jokingly. "Get used to it, sweetheart, you're yesterday's news now. There's literally a new kid in town," I yell over my shoulder before everyone mobs around me, wanting to see the baby.

Once we are all stuffed from filling our faces with Clark and Marty's delicious cooking, we move outside and sit around the fire pit. It's a beautiful night. Just the right temperature and a million stars shining in the sky. I love this. All of us just hanging out and talking. This is my idea of a perfect life.

Glancing over, I see Amber and Kyle smiling down at Cody. You can almost feel the love they have for him. It radiates. They look so happy. So Content. Like all is right in their world. Watching Amber with Cody makes me a little sad. It reminds me of something I lost once. Something I may never have the chance to have again. Before the building tears have a chance to spill over, I hear Amber gasp. When I look up, her hands are covering her mouth and her eyes are as big as saucers. I follow her gaze to see Paul down on one knee holding a black velvet box. At the sight, I feel a thousand butterflies flutter around inside my stomach. The tears already threatening to spill over do, and my hands are shaking so badly, I'm afraid everyone will notice. Not until this very moment had I realized how much I've wanted Paul to propose to me.

"Holly, before I met you, I was broken. I never thought I was capable of loving, let alone being loved. Then you showed up and knocked me flat on my ass. You've repaired a heart that was beyond repair. You saved me. I love you more than I will ever be able to tell you with mere words. Instead, let me show you, every day, for the rest of our lives. Will you marry me?" he asks, staring into my eyes. I can see how nervous he is as he waits for me to answer. I'm trying to get my voice to work, but I'm so emotional after those beautiful words, nothing will come out. Finally, I give up and start nodding my head yes, I must look psychotic. A huge smile spreads across Paul's face as he places the most beautiful ring I've ever seen on my finger. How could I not love this man when he knows me so well? This ring proves it. This ring screams me.

After wiping a tear from my eye with his thumb, he leans down and kisses me. It's the most passionate kiss I've ever experienced. If it weren't for all of the catcalls and whistles from our friends, I'd have forgotten we weren't alone.

"Remember where we left off. I'd like to pick it up in the exact same spot later," I tell him as we are both bombarded with congratulations. Amber comes flying across the room, screeching loudly. She throws her arms around me with such force, it sends us both tumbling to the floor. We're both laughing so hard, neither of us can get up. When I finally think I have it under control, I turn my head to look at Amber. And just like that, we start all over again. After a few more minutes, we get ourselves under control and off the floor.

"Ahh, why'd ya stop? I was enjoying watching you lovely ladies rolling around together on the floor," Angel jokes, earning himself not only one, but two slaps to the back of the head courtesy of Paul and Kyle. "Ouch. It's not like I asked to join them," he throws out as he runs away from another head slap.

I can honestly say this is the happiest I've ever been in my entire life. I'm surrounded by people who truly care about me, who I consider my family, and I'm going to marry my soulmate. It can't get any better than this. Nothing could ruin this moment. It's absolutely perfect. The doorbell rings and I wonder who it could be. Everyone we know is here.

"I'll get it," I yell on my way to the front door. As I approach the door, I'm hit with an eerie feeling that something's wrong. I don't know what it is or why I feel this way. I hate feeling uneasy.

It reminds me of a time when that's the only thing I felt. Never knowing what was coming next, but assured whatever it was wasn't good. That's a part of my life I've tried so hard to forget — ran so far away from, hoping never to see it again.

When I open the door, I realize I didn't run quite far enough. The air is knocked right out of my lungs when I see my ex-husband, Ray, standing before me.

5111

Made in the USA
Lexington, KY
03 March 2016